MW01487745

"Miss Jones but you were given as the main contact by one of our prisoners. I'd like to ask a few questions if I may."

"I assume you're calling about Ruby Jones." Ground coffee beans beckoned. A half cup of scalded frothy milk waited to join fresh-brewed espresso. Darn. Why didn't his call come in after I made coffee? I walked from the kitchen, blaming the man on the other end of the phone for my caffeine deprivation. "Ask away, Sheriff Gonzales."

"First, allow me to get you up to speed regarding last night's—uh—apparent homicide. I personally inspected the scene and made the arrest. Regarding the suspect, she is currently being—"

"Wait." I cut him off, mid-sentence. A high-pitched commotion in the background sounded all too familiar. "Is that Ruby?"

"*Un momento, por favor, Señorita* Jones."

A second tirade came across, loud and clear. "You can't do this to me! I have rights as an American citizen! Remember the Al-a-moooo!"

"*Cállate!*"

I smiled for the first time since the nightmare began. Good luck shutting Ruby up.

Margaritas, Mayhem & Murder

by

Mary Cunningham

An Andi Anna Jones Mystery, Book 1

Margaritas, Mayhem & Murder

COPYRIGHT © 2022 by Mary Kathleen Cunningham

Cover Art by *Abigail Owen*

The Wild Rose Press, Inc.
PO Box 708
Adams Basin, NY 14410-0708
Visit us at www.thewildrosepress.com

Publishing History
First Edition, 2022
Trade Paperback ISBN 978-1-5092-4108-8
Digital ISBN 978-1-5092-4109-5

An Andi Anna Jones Mystery, Book 1
Published in the United States of America

Dedication

To my rock, my buddy, my best friend and creative
sounding-board, my husband, Ken

Acknowledgments

To the fabulous group of writers at the Carrollton Writers Guild and Just Prose for their honest critiques—good and bad. To my first editor, Amber Pickle, whose thoughtful suggestions, editor's eye, and appreciation for Andi Anna Jones were invaluable. Heartfelt thanks to author/editor, Cheryl Tardiff, and to Karen Syed, who first took the chance on an inexperienced author many years ago.

How do I thank the perfect editor? Words can't begin to express my gratitude for editor Val Mathews, a supportive yet challenging taskmaster. Without her vision and discerning flair, this book would be filled with boring backstory. She immediately "got" the heroine's voice and sense of humor. I'm also thrilled and grateful my mystery is listed among the wide-ranging Wild Rose Press catalog.

To Diana Black, my life-long best friend. Andi Anna Jones wouldn't exist without her. To my husband, Ken. His criticism was as crucial to the development of this book as was his praise. And special thanks to beta readers, Mary, Kris, and Kit.

Finally, to Patty, Florida travel agency owner, who hired the worst agent this side of the Mississippi. Fortunately, my experience gathering inaccurate airline and hotel reservations gave voice, humor, and humility to Andi.

Chapter 1

I bolted upright, greeted by the wet, clammy sleeve of my faded unicorn nightshirt, and ripped off my sleep mask, along with a few strands of hair. *Oh, puh-leese. Who's calling at this un-godly hour?*

"Jeeze Louise!" I made a mental note: Don't set water glass on nightstand beside phone. *Speaking of which, where is the darn phone?* I made one more grab. Success!

"Hul-lo?" Tucking it under my chin, I patted my sleeve with the corner of the Egyptian cotton sheet I practically stole at a going out of business sale. Never too proud to sleep between bargain luxury.

"I said, *Hello!*"

Silence.

"Hey, jerk, you called me."

More silence.

"Okay, game over." My instincts kicked into high gear, and I was poised to bang the phone against the headboard. "If you're an obscene caller, better hold onto those eardrums—"

"Andi Anna, honey, is that you? Oh sugar, I'm so glad you answered!"

Andi Anna? Only two people on Earth used my middle name: my dearly departed dad, and...

"Ruby?"

I squinted at Dad's old alarm clock with its

illuminated hands. One of the few items I'd retrieved from the trash pile after his widow decided to dump everything that reminded her of "my dear, sweet Drew." Now to figure out why she was calling at two-thirty in the morning.

"Oh, yes honey, it's me, and oh, Andi Anna, I'm in truubble darlin'. Oh, land-sakes! I don't know what to do!" I held my phone at arm's length as the long-winded shriek came through.

I kicked my feet free of twisted linens, swung my legs over the side of the bed, and tapped my toes along the Mexican tile in search of my manatee slippers.

"Wait a minute, Ruby. Where are you? Shouldn't you be on a cruise ship in Cozumel?"

"Oh, Lordy, yes, but I had a little—" Ruby gasped. "—problem. I'm in Cancun, in the hoosegow."

The hoosegow? Surely not! On a good day, Ruby was a piece of work. Just when I got used to her theatrics, she'd raised them a notch. I was not, however, hearing her typical—lock the keys in the car with the engine running on the ferry to Fisher Island—hysteria. Something about this conversation was different.

"Andi Anna, are you still there? Hello?"

"Yes, I'm still here." Unfortunately. "So, tell me, how did you end up in a Cancun jail?"

"Some high-fallutin' sheriff, along with two of the rudest deputies in the whole wide world, ripped me right off the ship. One was even a woman!" Ruby scoffed. "She was the rudest of all. Can you believe it? I've never been so humiliated in my life. Why the whole ship watched while they marched me onto some stinky old ferry to the mainland, some tourist town called Carmen Miranda."

Carmen Miranda? I vaguely remembered my grandmother talking about an old-timey Broadway star by that name who wore fruit hats. Her nickname was the Brazilian Bombshell. Come to think of it, Granddad *really* liked her. Snort.

"Did you say something, Andi?"

"Uh, no. But this Carmen Miranda place, could that be Playa del Carmen?"

"You expect me to remember every single detail in my condition? I haven't told you the worst part. Soon as we got off that nasty boat, they dumped me into the back of a police car. You wouldn't believe the seats. Full of holes. Common criminals rode back there. I'm going to sue them six ways to Sunday, I can tell you. You don't humiliate Ruby Jones and get away with it."

"Okay, just calm down." Yeah, like that was going to happen. After the neighbor's beagle ripped to shreds the plastic flowers she'd planted around her lanai, it was a solid week before Ruby's breathing returned to normal. I calmed my voice and took a deep breath. "Tell me what's going on. Slowly and about fifty decibels lower. What are the charges?"

"Well, honey, I'm not sure. Oh, I know what they're saying, but I didn't do anything. I swear. Well, at least nothin' I can remember. You see, it all started on the cruise ship dance floor, quite innocently, mind you."

I found my slippers and shuffled to the bathroom in preparation for a long-winded dissertation. Catching a glimpse of my reflection in the wall mirror above the sink was my second mistake of the night. Answering the phone being the first. My sister was right. Without eyeliner and mascara, I had no eyes, whatsoever. They simply disappeared into a freckled blob that represented my too plump face. Not to be outdone, springy coils of sun-streaked hair stuck out like a dozen mini-slinkys. Don't get me wrong. I loved my dad, but why did I inherit his features instead of my mom's dark, classic looks?

"What started?"

"Why, Andi Anna, if I didn't know better, I'd believe you aren't even listening. It all started on the dance floor. You know, they play such romantic music on these cruises. Oh, don't you just love '70's crooners? Well, anyway, Lenny and I were having a lovely time, and he was obviously enamored, if you catch my drift."

I knew it was a mistake. Still, I asked, "Lenny who?"

"Why, Lenny La Mour, of course."

I drew a blank.

"Oh, you know who I'm taking about. Lenny La Mour, the famous Las Vegas performer? Why, he's the reason I picked this cruise. A few years back, he had his own humongous nightclub and everything. Don't tell me you've never heard of him. Why, every woman I know swoons at the sound of his voice. But I suppose your generation only has eyes for that Bon Ami person."

"Who in the world is Bon Ami?"

"Well, you know who I mean, that cute blond fella with the rock band."

"Please Ruby. I don't need a music quiz." Especially at oh-dark-thirty by my out-of-control, sixty-year-old, former stepmother. Her reputation to prattle on for hours and forget the purpose of the conversation was legendary. Waiting for her to take a breath, my mind wandered to possible reasons for Ruby's incarceration. Did she steal silverware from the captain's table? Jump on stage, grab a mike, and belt out a few show tunes? Honestly, she had no inhibition and certainly no filter when it came to putting herself on display.

I switched on the bathroom light while Ruby chattered on about dancing the Tango and how Lenny bent her over backward on the dance floor while her girlfriends whispered at their table.

"I'm telling you, Andi, they were all just green with envy."

I'll bet. I plopped down on the edge of my seldom-used garden tub—the one that took three hours and cost an arm and a leg to fill—and half-listened to her babble-thon. I heard enough disturbing details about her love life to consider selling everything I had in Miami and moving to a Tibetan monastery. My eyelids drooped as she droned on and on. Her voice, coupled with the early morning hour, proved more effective than a couple of sleeping pills. My right shoulder rested on the cool tile. My breathing slowed. I drifted off with the phone firmly planted against the wall and my ear. *Ah, this is nice...*

"Next thing I knew, after he'd gotten strapped into the climbing harness—"

"Whoa!" My head snapped to attention. I caught the phone a second before it hit the floor. "Stop right there. Did you just say something about a—"

Static filled the line. I voted that it was God's way of signaling it was time to hang up.

"Hey, you're breaking up, Ruby. Here's a thought.

Why not call your old buddy, Bert? You always say he's the best lawyer this side of the Mason-Dixon Line." Bert Bagley was not my favorite person. And lord knows, he couldn't even polish my late dad's shoes, let alone fill them. Still, Ruby seemed crazy about that particular ambulance chaser.

To my dismay, the static cleared. "Now, Andi Anna, I know you don't care much for Bert, but he's always there when I need him."

"So? Call him. As much as I want to help, there's really nothing a travel agent can do to get you out of jail."

"I tried but he wasn't home!"

Not home? In the middle of the night? So Bert-like. *Why can't I get a middle-of-the-night, run-of-the-mill, obscene phone call?*

That settled it. I looked skyward. *I know, Dad, I promised.* I couldn't leave his widow dangling on the other end of the phone, in another country. "Okay, calm down. It can't be that serious."

"Oh, Andi. I know we haven't seen eye-to-eye in the past, but I'll be forever grateful for your help, and I know dear, sweet Drew would be, too, God rest his soul." She sniffed.

I knew when to surrender. "What are the charges?"

A breathless whisper slithered through. "Murder."

Chapter 2

The call dropped, and I stared at the silent phone. Had I just heard Ruby say, "murder"?

No…no, that can't be. I was still groggy. Coffee. I needed coffee. I gave my hands a cursory wash, flipped off the bathroom light, and headed for the kitchen. It was a tossup whether exhaustion stemmed from lack of sleep or the conversation with Ruby. Talking to her bothered me to no end. She was nothing but drama, but this time there was actual fear in her voice. Sure, her description of the evening was all fun and games, so how did murder fit in? Whatever the case, I predicted a double shot of espresso in my imminent future.

My mood lifted a little as I ran my hand, expectantly, over the top of the cappuccino maker, stopping short of channeling my inner Tolkien, along with my Gollum impersonation. Every gulp of steaming gold was downright *precious*.

"It's a coffee monstrosity," Ruby had declared five years ago upon receiving the early wedding gift. "Give me a plain ol' cuppa Joe any day." Flipping the back of her hand in dramatic disdain, she'd added, "Andi, why don't you take it? Drew and I will never use such a complicated contraption." She didn't have to ask me twice.

I jumped when the phone rang in the middle of grinding beans. I weighed the options. Much-needed caffeine or my sense of duty? Duty won.

"Ruby?"

"Hello? Miss? Are you there?"

Well, this sure isn't Ruby. Nice baritone. "I'm here, but you're cutting out. Who's this?"

"Manuel Gonzales of the Cancun Sheriff's Department, Miss…"

"Jones. But then I imagine you already know since you called me." *Was this the high-fallutin' sheriff who arrested Ruby?*

"Miss Jones, I apologize for the early morning call, but you were given as the main contact by one of our prisoners. I'd like to ask a few questions if I may."

"I assume you're calling about Ruby Jones." Ground coffee beans beckoned. A half cup of scalded frothy milk waited to join fresh-brewed espresso. Darn. Why didn't his call come in after I made coffee? I walked from the kitchen, blaming the man on the other end of the phone for my caffeine deprivation. "Ask away, Sheriff Gonzales."

"First, allow me to get you up to speed regarding last night's—uh—apparent homicide. I personally inspected the scene and made the arrest. Regarding the suspect, she is currently being—"

"Wait." I cut him off, mid-sentence. A high-pitched commotion in the background sounded all too familiar. "Is that Ruby?"

"Un momento, por favor, Señorita Jones."

A second tirade came across, loud and clear. "You can't do this to me! I have rights as an American citizen! Remember the Al-a-moooo!"

"Cállate!"

I smiled for the first time since the nightmare

began. Good luck shutting Ruby up.

The screams became muffled. The sheriff's hand was either clasped over the phone or the perpetrator's mouth. I guessed the phone since his orders were muted. "Get Señora Loca out of here." He cleared his throat, I supposed to regain composure. "Sorry for yelling in your ear, Miss, but the suspect has been, uh, excitable since we brought her in."

I didn't doubt that, not one bit.

"Back to the reason for my call, she claims to be a relative of yours. Can you confirm this?"

"I…she's my former stepmother."

"Former? Does that mean you are no longer related?"

How do I answer? A clear "no" would have given me an out. But it went against Dad's wishes. "First, I'd like to know the exact charges."

Maybe I misunderstood the earlier conversation with Ruby. Did she get it wrong? I braced for his answer.

"I must advise that Señora Jones is charged with the very serious crime of murder."

My ears pounded like the beat of a base drum, eclipsed only by the troop of army ants marching up and down my spine. The image of Ruby strapped to an electric chair flashed before me. I slumped into the living room recliner.

Ruby's last skirmish with authority—getting tipsy and knocking a server and his entire tray of drinks into the Mangrove Hotel pool—moved down the list to a distant second. The server wasn't injured, but the three German tourists he fell on top of were. In addition, the pool had to be closed in the middle of a political fundraising cocktail party while glass was vacuumed from the bottom.

The hotel manager had every intention to let Ruby off with a simple warning, until she complained, loudly, about the Bloody Mary stain on her dress. "I'm the injured party here. Just look at my brand-new silk Valen-tiny-tino dress."

The fact she couldn't pronounce the name of the dress designer, nor stand for any length of time, didn't seal her fate. Her big mouth did. From what I had just heard, along with the sheriff's obvious frustration, she hadn't learned her lesson.

"Señorita, are you related to the suspect, or not?"

"Technically, no. She's my dad's widow, but my sister and I still consider her…family." At least Georgia did.

"So, she's correctly identified you as her next-of-kin. One more matter we need to discuss. Will you also assume legal responsibility for your ex-*madrastra*?"

"'Scuse me? Did you say, my ex-disaster?" Fitting label.

"*Perdón,* señorita, for my lapse. Your use of the title 'stepmother' is *madrastra,* in Spanish."

Disaster fit so much better.

"Señorita Jones, are you still there? I need your answer."

"Oh, yeah, you asked about legal responsibility. Sheriff Gonzales, I don't think clearly at 4:00 a.m. In fact, I don't think clearly at all when it comes to Ruby. Just to confirm, she is charged with murder."

"Si, and I'm about to add disturbing the peace. She insisted we play elevator music in her cell to calm her nerves. This is a jail, Miss Jones, not a fancy restaurant."

"I understand, sheriff." *Oh, how I understand.* There was something I didn't understand, however. "Uh, sheriff, since she was in Cozumel, how did she end up in the Cancun jail?"

"We are the largest jurisdiction in the state, Quintana Roo, and handle all hotel, cruise ship, and tourist-related crimes. I, and two other officers, apprehended the suspect early this morning and brought her to the mainland for processing."

Oh, Ruby, Ruby. What am I going to do with you? "Listen, sheriff, can I use the number on the caller-ID to get back to you? I need to let this soak in and put together some kind of plan."

"Si, señorita. I warn you, though. Do not take too long. I can't overstate the serious nature of this crime. The prosecutor has not made a determination between first and second-degree homicide, but Señora Jones will be held until her first court appearance."

"When will that be?"

"As soon as we can get her before the *juez*, uh, judge."

"In the meantime, is she comfortable? Is there anything she needs, Sheriff Gonzales?"

"We are well equipped to provide her necessities. As a matter of course, we make every effort to strictly care for and control our prisoners as peacefully and respectfully as possible without using restraints or solitary confinement. Your stepmother is testing those limits."

"I'm so sorry. She can be a handful, but she's usually harmless."

"Harmless?" He scoffed. "She has the entire jail in

turmoil from the guards to the prisoners."

I pictured guards running for their lives and inmates cowering in their cells during one of her outbursts.

"Besides—"

I pictured him wagging his finger.

"—may I remind you of the charges?"

"No need. I haven't forgotten." Before hanging up, I, again, murmured my sympathies for his having to deal with Ruby. "I'll get back to you by late morning. You have my word."

I hung up mad at the sheriff, mad at Dad for putting me in stepmother protector role, mad at myself for answering the damned phone in the first place, and most of all, "Ruby, what the hell have you done?"

While grinding beans for my first coffee of the day, I glanced at the bookshelf situated on the wall just outside the kitchen. A picture of my mother, around age twenty, caught my eye. Carla Alvero Jones's looks typified her Italian heritage. She was poised, calm, eloquent even. It's no wonder I'd had such a visceral dislike of Ruby, the polar opposite of my quietly classy mother. Five years ago, when Dad said he'd met a "firecracker redhead" at the Hialeah Bingo Palace, I'd tried to warn my sister Georgia, we were all in for trouble.

"Bingo, Georgia? You had to suggest Dad try his hand at bingo? Can you see our mother staring at a half-dozen cards waiting for B-6 to be called?"

"Mom's gone, "Georgia said. "She's been gone for years. Deal with it."

"I know, I know."

The placid expression in my mother's picture

belied a volatile, though random, temper. Mother could rip you to shreds in an argument, but normally relied on soft-spoken requests to get her way. Another trait Georgia inherited. Flash temper, aside, never, ever would either one commit murder.

Ruby, on the other hand…

Hoping to catch my breath, think, and most of all, relax, I loaded my coffee with all the good stuff and raised my mug in a mock salute. "Here's to you, Ruby, and to whatever god-awful mess you've gotten yourself into."

I opened the door leading to the small patio attached to my condo. Maybe a little peace and quiet and fresh air would clear my head. *Man, it's hot!* Not only that, the table and chairs were soaked with early morning dew, and street noise cluttered the air. "Where are all these people going at five in the morning?" The nearby highway was jammed with honking cars and revving engines. So much for quiet contemplation.

I grabbed my coffee, stepped back inside, and shut the door. "Cooler in here, anyway." You'd think an honest-to-goodness Florida native would be used to heat and humidity after thirty-six years. Must be true, the older you get the less tolerant you become to heat, noise, and drama.

I stared at the creamy goodness inside my over-sized coffee mug and wished Ruby had made her one frantic, middle-of-the-night phone call to someone else. Someone like Georgia, who might have empathy toward her and the situation. That's it! She'd always seen the good, or at least tolerable, side of our stepmother. I grabbed my cell and punched number two on speed dial.

"Andi? What's wrong?"

"Hey, sis! How ya doing?"

"How am I doing? It's not even 5:00 a.m. Have you been in a wreck? Are you in the hospital? Oh, don't tell me you got arrested again!"

"Slow down, Georgia. I've never been arrested. Not officially. Anyway, I was within my rights to blast my car horn in the bank drive-up lane. That snotty teller at the window, saying I couldn't—"

"You were trying to cash a third-party check, Andi. From Guatemala, for heaven's sake. You're thirty-six years old. It's time to grow up."

Oh, here we go, again. My baby sister was always telling me to grow up. I fought the urge to lash out like when we were kids. Timing, Andi, timing. "I'm not calling to talk about me. It's Ruby. She's in jail. In Cancun. And get this—" I paused for effect. "—she's been charged with murder."

"Nice talking to you, Andi. Call again sometime, but when you're sober."

"I'm perfectly sober! Don't hang up. I'm guessing you're up with the baby anyway."

"Yes, and he was just drifting off when you called."

Hmm, I guessed right. Don't mistake my sarcasm. I loved Georgia dearly, and doted on my nieces and nephews, but admitted a tad bit of jealously when it came to her hectic but satisfying family life. She had a devoted husband and four kids, the conception of the last being a total shock.

"You do know how that happens, right?" I remember being unable to resist teasing my frustratingly organized (to the brink of OCD) sister when her perfect family plans turned a bit imperfect.

"Listen, Andi. I'm sure this is important, but I have to get Marcus back to bed. If not, he'll sleep all day and keep me up all night. Call in the morning."

"It is morning, sis."

"Call back when it's late morning. And Andi, I do mean late."

"Please, Georgia. Don't hang up. This is serious. When have you ever known me to be up this early?"

"Voluntarily or involuntarily? Are we counting all those college dorm keggers?"

"Georgia, please!"

"Give me a break. You can't be serious about our stepmother murdering someone on the birthday cruise you arranged. Are you sure it wasn't one of those murder-mystery dealies? I could see Ruby getting caught up in theatrics."

"I agree she's not the sharpest knife in the drawer, but no. I got it straight from the horse's mouth and also straight from the Cancun sheriff, whom I might add has one of the sexiest voices I've ever heard."

"Oh, good lord."

"This is why Ruby needs someone who's level-headed. We'd all be better off if you'd take over this little stepmommy murder matter."

"You mean you'd be better off, right?"

She had me there. "It's just that when it comes to Ruby, I'm not sure why either of us should get involved, except for, you know, guilt since Dad asked us to watch after her."

"No, Andi. Heaven only knows why, but our father asked you to watch after her."

Oh, so Georgia's going to play dirty, huh? I saw

right then it would take my big sis manipulating skills to convince her to take Ruby off my to-do list, or at least help with the situation. "You've always been so good with the old broad, er, dear Ruby. Please, just listen."

I spilled every detail of the conversation with Sheriff Gonzales, and she listened without saying a word.

"That's it. Knowing Ruby's cantankerous personality, they're probably constructing gallows as we speak."

"Always the drama queen, Andi. They don't hang women in Mexico for simply being irritating...even though Ruby takes irritation to a whole new level."

"If that were the only charge."

"Despite all her annoying habits, I refuse to believe Ruby's capable of murder. Since I'm wide awake anyway, along with Marcus, let's put our heads together, and come up with a plan."

Chapter 3

Funny how *our* plan turned into *my* trip to Mexico.

I shifted in my seat, wishing I could sleep, but constant turbulence threatened a reappearance of the beef and bean burrito I'd grabbed on the way to the Miami airport.

After hanging up with Georgia, I grudgingly admitted she couldn't possibly fly out of the country leaving four kids with Javier. Don't get me wrong. He was an attentive father, no question, but completely helpless when it came to the common-sense basics of raising kids. Just last week, he'd fed paella to Marcus with disastrous consequences.

"TMI, Georgia," I'd protested during her vivid description of the clean-up.

I dug through my bag and gave my travel assistant, Ellie, props for reminding me to pack a Spanish dictionary. Off the top of my head, I recalled a few practical phrases from one semester of high school Spanish: *Buenos dias? Cómo está usted.* I also understood the sheriff's frustrated order to remove Ruby from the room. In other words, I was sunk if the conversation went too far beyond "How are you?" or "Good day."

"Would you like a drink, Miss?" The smiling flight attendant plopped ice cubes in a plastic glass and waited for my decision.

"How about a Bloody Mary? On second thought, better make that coffee, and keep it coming." As inviting as slugging down a little tomato juice and a lot of vodka sounded, I needed to stay sharp. Suppose Ruby did kill someone? My stomach churned. Right on cue, the plane dipped, and the flight attendant grabbed onto the back of my seat. Oh, why did I have that burrito?

Slurps of black coffee brought my focus to the flight magazine in the seat pocket. Land of 10,000 Lakes graced the cover reminding me of the last trip Dad and I took to our cabin in Minnesota. "I love this place" was always the first phrase out of his mouth. It was his sanctuary. Even a kid could see the peace that came over him. The decision to sell hadn't been easy. But when Mom got sick, Dad lost interest. He told me that family took priority over a piece of land or a wooden structure.

So, there you had it. Along with family came responsibility. Lesson learned. Wish we could've stayed at thirty-five thousand feet and cruised forever so I could avoid my family responsibility.

More turbulence. Urp. That's all I needed. It was hard enough being strapped into a confined tube and having to breathe through my claustrophobia.

Finally! The timely thump of the landing gear engaged. Anxious thoughts and a nervous stomach diminished as the Yucatan landscape came into view. Hard to believe all that scrubland led to a tropical paradise of hotels, palm trees, and white sandy beaches. Whatever the welcoming sight of a runway meant, we would soon land. I closed my eyes and exhaled when the tires hit the ground.

The moment the plane made the turn to taxi toward the gate, I jumped into the aisle and grabbed my carry-on from the overhead bin. The seat Ellie booked at the back of the plane was convenient with easy access to the lavatory. Hmmm, so close, yet I didn't use it. Now that I wanted—no needed—to exit as quickly as possible, I was trapped. Stupid tourists blocked the aisle ahead of me and behind me. Why weren't we moving? Uh-oh. Clammy hands. Dry mouth. My claustrophobia was kicking into high gear. Would that guy in the red-flowered shirt ever move his butt? Breathe. Breathe. Where's a Bloody Mary when you need it?

That did it! One more second and I'd lose my marbles. No choice but to push my way off this flying circus. "Coming through, coming through. Oh, sorry. Didn't realize that was your foot, sir."

Finally on the ramp, I breathed in a small trace of late-afternoon air—stifling, at best. No need to waste time in baggage claim. I'd packed light, as usual. The airport was fairly small so following signs to the exit was simple, especially since they were in Spanish and English.

Salida. Exit. Yep, even I could translate that.

Before leaving the States, I'd notified Sheriff Gonzales of my arrival time but didn't think there was a chance in Hades anyone would meet me. I dug in my purse for my phone. I needed to ask Ellie to look up the police station's address. Guess I could've looked it up myself, but misplaced guilt for leaving so abruptly compelled me to check on the business. One phone call and then I'd hunt for a restroom. I pushed number one on speed dial.

"Señorita Jones?"

It wasn't Ellie. I checked the number on the screen. Yep, I'd called the agency. Listening to the still ringing phone, I grumbled, "C'mon and answer, El."

A tall man in a uniform stepped forward, sliding a pair of aviator sunglasses to the top of a full head of dark brown hair. "Pardon the interruption. Are you Miss Jones?"

My gaze locked onto smoky hazel eyes. And I do mean locked. "Ye-yesss. I'm Miss Jones. But how did you know?"

"Oh, we have our ways." The corners of his mouth turned up, and he pointed to his badge. "I'm Sheriff Gonzales. We spoke on the phone."

I got nothing. Total loss for words. Even my wildest dreams couldn't have conjured this square-jawed, golden-skinned Mayan god straight out of a GQ Magazine. For the first time since this nightmare began, I wanted to fall to my knees and say, thank you, thank you, thank you, Ruby.

"I was already in the area on official business and finished in time to meet your flight. I'm parked at the curb. May I take your bag?"

I blinked a couple of times to be sure he wasn't a mirage. "What? No, thank you, Sheriff. I can handle it myself. I appreciate the ride, but I could've taken a taxi, you know."

"Hello…hello, Jonesy, are you there?"

The sheriff scrunched a set of perfect masculine eyebrows. "I believe your call has been answered."

"What? I…sorry, wrong number." I disconnected, figuring I'd call Ellie later and explain. She'd understand when I described the hunk standing before me.

"I apologize if you thought I doubted your competence, Miss Jones, but considering the stressful nature of the situation, I thought it best if someone picked you up. Finding transportation into the city can be confusing."

My subconscious longed to blurt out "you might be the most handsome man I've ever seen in my entire life." With every ounce of strength I could muster, I coolly stated, "Cancun's transportation system might be confusing for the average tourist, but I'm a travel agent, perfectly capable of finding my way into and around the city."

Adjusting the strap of my carryon bag, I tossed my head and walked into the side of a trashcan.

The ride from the airport to the *Policia Quintana Roo* took longer than expected. Tourist traffic, buses, and transport vehicles clogged the only road to the hotel district. My bladder wasn't talking; it was screaming. Nice move ignoring the lavatory right behind my plane seat. The second we stopped, I excused myself, jumped from the car, and dashed inside. Panicked, I searched the hallway. Where was the danged ladies room? Did they even have one? Halfway down the main hall I spotted a sign with an arrow pointing left. *Cuarto de baño*. Hey. Another Spanish phrase I knew.

After taking care of business, I stood at the sink washing my hands. My reflection in the mirror signaled a different emergency. Dark circles and smeared mascara, along with the dazzling vision of Sheriff Gonzales, called for a drastic makeup overhaul.

"You're just a nature gal, Andi," Dad used to say and then tease me about the annoying freckles that sprang from the South Florida sun despite diligent use of sixty-plus sunscreen. "Don't fight it," he'd add with a tender rub on my cheek. "You're the image of your Grammy."

I smiled in the mirror thinking how I used to make a game of counting the freckles on my paternal grandmother's face. *Speaking of the deceased, when, in the name of King Tut's mummy, did I get all these frown lines?* I dabbed concealer under my eyes, glossed my lips, checked my teeth for lingering bits of that beef and bean burrito, and switched gears for the task ahead.

"Hope I'm up to this, Dad."

Chapter 4

"Miss Jones?" The sheriff waited at the doorway to his office. "I trust you located the, uh, accommodations. Please, come in."

"Sorry for running off like that." I spared the details concerning the gallon of coffee I consumed on the plane, and the fact I was feeling too claustrophobic to use the plane's facilities.

"No apology necessary." He offered a seat. "So, your name is really Andi Anna Jones? Is there a story?"

Here we go, again. I settled in the straight-back chair and prepared, for the umpteenth time, to explain. For as long as I could remember, I'd enjoyed throwing people off about my name's origin. "I suppose you've heard of *Raiders of the Lost Arc* with—"

"Oh, yes!" Sheriff Gonzales snapped the air with a pretend bullwhip. "Indiana Jones!"

I mentally cast the sheriff in the lead role to rave reviews.

"Just kidding," I said and smirked at the confusion on his face. "I was named after my dad. A flawed ultrasound convinced my parents they were having a boy, Andrew Anderson Jones III. Can you imagine their shock when a curly-headed girl appeared? With my dad still insisting on a namesake and my mother insisting I have a proper girl's name, they compromised. The rest is, uh, family history."

"So, Andrew Anderson turned into Andi Anna." The sheriff took a seat behind the desk. "I understand why a boy's name would not suit you in the least."

That bedroom gaze penetrated my body like laser beams.

"However, I also get your father's point. Either way, your name is one that won't soon be forgotten, especially by me."

Heat rose from my chest to my cheeks. I turned my head and pretended to cough, trying to cover my self-conscious attraction to the man sitting across from me. Fortunately, he moved on seamlessly with the conversation, and I was off the hook.

"Do you mind if I call you Andi? You may call me Manny if you'd like. Most people do." It was his turn to appear uncomfortable. Tiny sweat-beads popped across his upper lip.

So, I wasn't the only one experiencing a bit of tension. "Andi will be fine." My voice cracked. Sparks were definitely bouncing off the walls like swarms of light-seeking moths.

He shuffled papers on his desk, while I glanced, subtly, at his left hand for signs of a wedding band. Nope, none there. Not even a hint of a tan line. I smiled with a smidge of satisfaction.

A smidge too noticeable. Manny looked down and spread the fingers on his left hand. "Do you find my hand amusing?"

I tried, unsuccessfully, to curb another blush. "Oh, no, really your hand is just fine. I just remembered something funny my assistant said before I left Miami." Please, oh, please don't ask. An insistent knock on the glass door broke the awkward silence. Whew!

"*Perdone mí*, Manny. *Aquí está el informe que usted solicitó.*"

"*Si. Gracias, Luis.*"

The sheriff appeared as relieved by the interruption as I. He took a manila folder from Luis, opened it, and read to himself.

Squinting, I barely made out a name on the tab: *Ruby Jones.* Mental note: Make appointment with optometrist in Miami. "Is that information on the case?" I asked. "What does it say?"

Manny ignored the questions and continued to read, flipping through page after page after page.

Maybe it was lack of sleep, or increasing stress, but my patience got thinner by the minute. "How can a crime that happened less than twenty-four hours ago take up so much paper? Don't you have computers around here?"

He settled back in his chair, all business. "I understand your frustration, but as I mentioned on the phone, your stepmother put on quite a show last night. The case against her is rather detailed and grows by the hour."

I jumped to my feet and got right in his face. Big mistake. The scent of his cologne—citrus and spiced rum—stopped me mid-thought, but I fought through the urge to swoon like a southern belle. Instead, I channeled my best steel magnolia. "What details? I don't even know the man she's accused of murdering." A small lie, but who was counting?

"His name is...*was* Lenny La Mour. He was a—"

"I know. I know. A lounge singer. I did get that much out of Ruby this morning." I paced the small room. This wasn't good. Not good at all. Ruby had admitted spending most of the evening with the victim but swore he was alive the last time she saw him. Chin up, arms crossed, I quizzed the sheriff. "Why is Ruby the only suspect? Were there any witnesses connecting her to Mr. La Mour?"

Manny waved the folder. "A room full of people saw them leave the lounge together. A female server delivering an order to the victim's cabin heard a violent argument through the door between Señora Jones and Señor La Mour. According to the employee's account, your stepmother opened the door, snatched the tray of food, and screamed, 'Get out of my sight.' "

Much as I criticized Ruby, I couldn't picture the scene. "That doesn't sound like her. As annoying as she can be, I've never seen her blow up like that. She's a master manipulator, sure, but obnoxious schemers don't necessarily commit murder, do they?"

"Did your stepmother happen to tell you how Señor La Mour died?"

"She never got the chance. I told you we were disconnected." Hazel eyes or not, he was starting to piss me off.

"The couple illegally accessed a closed area of the ship. Well-after dark. According to a witness in the lounge, your stepmother had bullied the victim about confronting his fear of heights on the rock-climbing wall, one of the sports-related activities available on ship. Several hours later, he was found hanging in the harness about halfway up—dead."

I reeled at the mental picture. Placing my palms on the desk for balance, I asked, "Who saw them leave the lounge together, and who found him?"

Manny didn't bat an eye. "A security guard,

checking the locks, found La Mour. Our investigation turned up two sets of fingerprints on the gate: your stepmother's and the victim's. As to the witness in the lounge, I can only say it was a passenger at your stepmother's table. According to the timeline provided by Señora Jones, La Mour and she left the climbing wall and activity deck together around 2:00 a.m. and said 'goodnight' at her cabin. Her cabin mate contradicts the time."

"Her cabinmate? Ethel Lipton? Is she the witness?"

"Yes, I can't give out witnesses' names. The timeline suggests your stepmother arrived back at her cabin several hours later than she acknowledged."

I flopped, wearily, into the chair. Ruby, Ruby, Ruby. I was at my wit's end with information overload when my cell buzzed. "Sorry, may I get this?"

The sheriff nodded.

"Andi? That you, sweetheart?"

"Yeah, Bert."

"Wuzzup? I got this frantic message on my answering machine from Ruby, but she's not answering her phone. Did she get seasick and fall overboard?"

He let loose one his patented laughs, and I pulled the phone from my ear. Heat crept up my neck again but this time from raw anger. Was there anyone more obnoxious than Bert Bagley?

"No, Bert. As a matter of fact, she's sitting in a Cancun, Mexico jail. So, lose the donkey bray. I'm not in the mood."

"Donkey what? Wait, what did you just say? What happened?"

"Ruby's in J-A-I-L in Cancun, and since you're her lawyer…"

Bert sucked in a deep breath. "Gee, I'm not officially her lawyer. I'll do what I can, Andi, but my schedule's awfully full for the next, uh, month, or three."

I stood abruptly, my teeth clinched, and cupped my hand around the phone. "You get your weasel butt down here now, or you know what."

"Uh, what?"

"I might have to call Judge Horton and mention the bribe you took from that exotic bird importer. Think the authorities would be interested in how you got your rare yellow-headed parrot?"

"Now, A-Andi, I found that silly ol' bird sitting in my palmetto tree, just looking for a home. What makes you think Chico came from an importer?"

"Ruby told me."

Bert swore under his breath but recovered. "Oh, that Ruby. Always the kidder. Tell ya what. I'll be down there on the next plane. Wouldn't want our little gal spending one extra second in lockup. Just have to check whether my Mexican law license is up to date."

"I thought you might see it that way." Once a sleaze, always a sleaze. Why I'd even want him in the same country was a mystery. Perhaps to babysit? "Take a taxi when you get here, Bert. Ask for the Cancun jail on the main hotel drag."

I hung up half-hoping he'd be his usual underhanded self and stay in Miramar. Dealing with the likes of him, in addition to Ruby, might be the last straw. Still, what choice did I have? I needed legal advice, even if it came in the form of a washed-up lawyer.

"Good news?" Manny's voice snapped me out of

my bad mood when I returned to his office.

"Well, news, at least." I muted the ringer on phone and slipped it back in my purse. "Ruby's lawyer says he'll be on the next flight. Could be good or bad, depending on how many Salty Dogs he has on the plane. Now, I think you left off with Lenny's body swinging from a harness."

He shut the folder and scooted his chair back from the desk. "Perhaps we both need a break from crime scene details. Let's move to something less gruesome. Will you give me some background information on your stepmother, er, ex-stepmother?"

"Do you want the good, the bad, or the ugly?"

I crossed my legs and straightened the white poly-blend skirt I wore when I traveled. The sheriff glanced downward but quickly looked up, appearing to study the grungy ceiling tiles. Tapping nervous fingers on the desk, he asked. "Now, what exactly was she doing in Cozumel?"

Good. A generic question I could answer, truthfully without perjuring Ruby or me. "She asked me to book a cruise for her sixtieth birthday. Oh, but please don't say I mentioned her age. She'll kill me."

"I won't breathe a word, although that is already in the official report. Continue, please." He looked up and I forgot, for a moment, where I was. "Andi? Would you continue?"

"Oh! Yes, of course." Deep breath. "Ruby asked me to book a tour for her and three friends—Bunco buddies from years back. She'd always wanted to go to Cancun but didn't like flying so I found her a cruise.

I decided, for the moment, to keep to myself that Ruby may have wanted that specific cruise because

Lenny was performing. She may have already spilled that little tidbit, but I wasn't going to be the one to give them reason to add premeditation to the charge.

"I'm a travel agent," I added, for the second or third time.

He smiled. "Yes, I know."

"Sure you do," I muttered. "Would you mind telling me what I had for dinner last night?" *Oh, geesh, Andi, stop trying to make such lame jokes.*

Thankfully, the sheriff ignored my weak sarcastic attempt and leaned back against the wall. Rolling an ink pen between his thumb and forefinger, he asked, "These friends of Señora Jones, are they close friends? Would any of them have a grudge against her?"

I meant to laugh but snorted instead. "Oops, sorry. Your question has a complicated answer. They act like they're joined at the hip, but Ruby said, more than once, she wouldn't trust a couple of those backstabbing old biddies. Poor choice of words. Why do you ask?"

"Although somewhat hesitant to talk, one of those friends gave great detail linking your stepmother to Señor La Mour's murder. The cabin mate I mentioned earlier was reluctant to talk but described a scene in the lounge during which the accused 'joked about the victim's fear of heights.' According to other witnesses, he was reluctant, but Mrs. Jones was quite insistent he needed to get over his fear. Does that sound like her?"

Insistent? Oh, yeah, that's Ruby, along with aggressive and demanding. You could add man-crazy to the list. But I said, "That doesn't sound like the Ruby I know."

Lying to the police. I knew I'd better watch out or I'll be in the hoosegow next to dear stepmom.

"Well," I said, "it sounds more like the witness was a little jealous that Lenny left with another woman."

Could be some truth to my statement. Ethel Lipton's face had the appearance of an over-ripe avocado. I'd heard, more than once, she was jealous of Ruby's appeal, at least to old farts.

"But that friend was not the only witness." Leaning forward, his elbows on the desk, the sheriff shrugged his muscular shoulders. "The woman who delivered the room service tray also delivered the most damning evidence. Do you recognize this?"

He held out a plastic bag. Inside was a white handkerchief with the name *Ruby* embroidered in red. I immediately recognized it as one of the dozen or so hankies Dad gave her their first Christmas together. An old-fashioned gift in this day and time, but she always carried one in her purse. "Yeah, it looks like one of Ruby's. So?"

"A housekeeper found this in the hallway outside the sports complex door. Wrapped inside was a small amount of bee pollen. Coincidentally, a bracelet was found on Señor La Mour's wrist, indicating he was highly allergic to anything having to do with bees—stings, pollen, and even honey. When he was found, his throat was swollen shut and his lips were three times their normal size."

My image of the crime scene sped into hyper-drive. I wanted no more grisly details until I heard Ruby's side of the story. "Sheriff, can we continue this later? I'd like to see my stepmother. Now."

Chapter 5

Ruby ran full tilt through the door of the dimly lit visitation room. I held out my arms in self-defense. Despite my best efforts, she screamed, pinned my arms to my sides, and squeezed the breath out of me. I gasped.

"Oh, thank the Lord you're here! What am I gonna dooo!"

"First," I said, "Let. Me. Go."

She stepped back and added bawling to the list of responses. I studied the emotional wreck standing before me and questioned if I was up to the task my dad had bestowed.

I summoned every ounce of patience. "C'mon Ruby. That's not going to help." I pulled a linty tissue from my purse and handed it to the sobbing woman.

"Oh, thank you, hon." *Honk. Sniff, Honnnk.* "I'm okay. As long as I don't think about poor Lenny. Oh, my poor, sweet Lenny."

That did it. Patience had limits. I grabbed Ruby by the shoulders. "Snap out of it. You barely knew the guy."

Her tears shut off instantly. "Well! You don't have to be rude." She dabbed at streaks of mascara, and tried, unsuccessfully, to straighten her flea market hairpiece.

Why in the world did they let her keep that monstrosity on her head? She could hide a grenade inside that mop.

"Oh, I'll bet I'm a sight."

I bit my lip to keep from answering honestly and called for strength from any higher power willing to help. "Sorry, Ruby. Didn't mean to upset you. I know you're scared, but you need to calm down if we're going to figure this out."

She produced a final loud honk and thrust the well-used tissue in my direction.

"Uh, no thanks. You can keep it." I cupped her elbow and led her to an empty table and chairs in the middle of the room. "I'm just trying to find out what happened. Whenever you're ready. I'm sure this is difficult, but you need to concentrate." *Please make it soon.* "Start from the beginning and try to remember every last detail."

She sat, glumly, on one side of the table and twisted the tissue into the shape of a white licorice stick. I settled on the opposite side, my knee bouncing nervously. It was clear we weren't used to serious one-on-one discussions. In fact, it might have been the first one we'd ever had. Even at Dad's funeral, I steered clear of Ruby's drama queen antics. Oh, sure, the widow had a right to be grief-stricken; nevertheless, she played her part to the hilt, making the most of every sympathetic ear she could bend.

"Drew was the love of my life," she had sobbed at the casket, stroking the forehead of my dad's corpse until I thought I would scream.

He didn't even want an open casket. "Just take me out back and start a bonfire," he'd told Georgia and me. "Hell, roast marshmallows and hot dogs, if you want." No, our dad wanted nothing like the pomp and circumstance—room overflowing with funeral bouquets and potted plants—Ruby had demanded.

I snapped back from the worst day in my life to perhaps the second worst.

Ruby spilled details in the style of a Broadway play production. "As I told you on the phone last night—" She paused, pursing collagen-augmented lips. "That was you I was talking to, right?"

I sighed. "It was. Just for the record, it was early morning." Speaking of early morning, the realization I'd been awake, going full speed, for a full day hit like a ton of bricks. Concentrating on Ruby's tale would be a challenge, but I didn't waste time and money flying to Mexico for nothing. "Sorry to interrupt."

"Alrighty then, where was I?" She staged a dramatic huff. "Oh, yes. Lenny and I were having the most wonderful time—dancing, singing, and gazing deeply in each other's eyes." Her arms swayed back and forth, and she stared dreamily into space.

I had to bring her back.

"Everyone could see we were so into each other. In fact, around midnight, he whispered in my ear that he wanted to get away from the crowd and take a stroll around the deck. I whispered back that I thought a stroll was a perfect way to end the evening. He gave a devilish little laugh and said, 'Did I mention anything about ending the evening?' That's when he pulled me close and asked if I'd like to go to the midnight buffet or would I prefer ordering in." She, again, took on that faraway look.

I tapped the back of her hand. "Earth to Ruby. Earth to Ruby. So, that's where you went? Straight back to his cabin?"

"Not directly. Land sakes! We went the long way around the deck of the ship. Oh, my! It was such a perfect evening, Andi. Full moon and thousands of stars." She gasped and covered her mouth.

"What is it?" I grabbed her elbow. "Did you remember something important?"

"Oh, dear." Her lips pursed like a sad clown. "Here I am going on and on about romance, and you're all alone. You simply must find a fella to take you dancing and partying. That's how a young woman should spend her vacation."

"Ruby, have you forgotten? I'm not here on vacation. You're in jail, and I flew, at great expense, to get you out, if possible."

Within an inch of leaving her to her own devices, or demise, I considered how it would look and feel. I imagined Georgia badgering me the rest of my life and Dad haunting me for abandoning his widow. So, I plodded on.

"Did you make any stops?" I asked. "Witnesses say, before you two left, you were hassling Lenny into trying some dangerous stunt."

"The climbing wall? Oh, for goodness' sake! That isn't dangerous. At least it's not supposed to be. Besides, he simply mentioned a fear of heights, and I thought tackling that wall would be the perfect opportunity to get over it. No way did I badger him. You know me better than that. Why, I believe in live and let live. Oh, I guess that's not a very appropriate thing to say, under the circumstances."

No, it wasn't, but typical of Ruby's way with words.

"In fact, Lenny even challenged me to try climbing

that wall, too."

"And did you?"

"Patience," she huffed. "I'll get to that in due time."

I sat back, resigned that the only way to achieve progress was to let Ruby be Ruby. She never could get straight to the point, and the series of events that led to a man's death, would be no exception. "Okay, so what happened, next? Did you go to his place?"

She giggled. "Oh, yes and was it ever extravagant. Private balcony and a huge shower. Why his bathroom was bigger than my whole cabin." She threw open her arms and flung the grungy tissue across the room. "Anyway, after we settled in, we ordered room service. I wasn't all that hungry, but Lenny had his heart set on raw oysters. You know they're supposed to be an aphrodite."

Her pencil-drawn eyebrows bounced devilishly on her forehead.

Aphrodite? What in the world? *Ah-ha.* "You mean aphrodisiac."

The correction flew right over her head. "He ordered a Mexican cocktail for me. I'd never had one, but when he told me what was in it—shrimp, tomato and clam juice, horseradish, avocado, and a bunch of other stuff—it sounded heavenly. Oh, and did I tell you about the champagne? He ordered a very expensive bottle, and then we talked about what kind of trouble we could get into after dinner."

Trouble? Now we're getting to the heart of the matter. "So, did you?"

"Did we what, sugar?"

Oh, for Pete's sake. "Get into trouble!" Did I really

want to know? A better question: how much longer could I sit there without strangling her?

"Please stop interrupting." She tossed her head, loosening a couple of pins that held that awful hair piece in place. Did she realize she was under suspicion for murder? Or did she think we were there to gossip about a date? I didn't know which was preferable. I'd never witnessed Ruby accurately processing real and present danger.

She continued the timeline of events much like a teenage girl at a slumber party. "We waited for our meals to come. Lenny was just famished. Anyway—Andi, are you listening?"

"Hmm? Yes, sure. Lenny was famished."

She gazed at the ceiling and tapped her cheek with her index finger. "It took almost an hour but, finally, we heard a knock on the cabin door. Lenny answered, took the tray, and handed the server a very generous tip. She said, 'Grassy-ass,' and Lenny shut the door."

That sounded nothing like the witness statement I'd heard from the sheriff. "This waitperson, male or female?"

"She was definitely female. Come to think of it, there was something strange about her." Ruby leaned back and frowned "I just saw her for a minute or two, but she had this funny look in her eyes, almost mean, nasty. I got the shivers when she gave me the once-over for what I considered a rude amount of time. And Lenny must've noticed too because his hands shook a little when he set the tray of food on the table. At first, I thought he was distracted by those bosoms of hers squishing out of her uniform for all to see. She was almost as well-endowed as yours truly."

I ignored her self-aggrandizing. "Did he say anything after she left? Do you think he'd seen her before?" I didn't like making snap judgements about people. Picturing Lenny flirting with one of the ship's employees wasn't much of a stretch. Oh, who was I kidding? Within twenty seconds, I either liked you or I didn't.

"Oh, nooo," Ruby said. "He was fine after a bit. Got frisky and everything. But I have to admit those evil eyes of hers are planted in my brain."

Hmph, good to know something lives in there besides cobwebs and marbles. "But you and Lenny went out after that," I reminded her. "Since his body wasn't found in the cabin."

She sucked in a breath. "Yes, his body."

She sighed, possibly to clear away negative images of the evening.

"Well, after we ate, he suggested another moonlight stroll. You know, to get our digestive systems going." She tapped the back of my hand. "Now that you and I are middle aged, we have to watch that, you know."

Thanks for including me in your age group, Ruby. "So, you went out after you ate?"

"Yes, although I was a little disappointed that we didn't spend more time in the cabin." She drifted off, again.

"Ruby!"

"Huh? Oh, anyway, we were about halfway around the deck, again, when I remembered the wall-climbing adventure. I'm sure he hoped I'd forgotten." She snickered. "It was one deck above us."

"And you went there with him? Did anyone else

see you?" While I did my best to make sense of Ruby's recollection of events from the previous night, I wished I'd thought to hit record on my phone. As it was, I scribbled a couple of notes as she talked but had to rely on my memory as well.

According to her account, when they reached the sports deck, Lenny slid the pass key in the lock. She remembered a tiny beam blinked from red to green, and the gate swung open.

She mentioned how the humidity hit her like a wet sponge. "Do you know what that does to my hair?"

"Yes, finish the story."

"I turned to Lenny and whispered, 'Are you sure we won't get caught?' " She giggled like a teenager skinny-dipping at a moonlit beach party. "Lenny puffed out his chest and reassured me. 'Not to worry, my little gem.' That's what he called me. You know—ruby-gem."

"Yeah, I get it. Clever."

"Anyway," she continued. "With a bottle of champagne, which I swear cost more than my monthly rent, securely tucked under his arm, he gave me a very satisfied smile. 'I've greased so many palms tonight,' he said, 'we're guaranteed an exciting, private evening.' I playfully slapped him on the shoulder of his dashing, flamingo-pink dinner jacket. Oh, he looked so handsome. Anyway, I said, 'You're so bad.' That means I thought he was *so good*, Andi."

"Yes, Ruby. I understand that." Geesh. "Please, go on."

"Well, the gate clanked shut behind us, and we had to stop until our eyes adjusted to that dark sports deck. The wave pool at the far end was our only light. Lenny motioned for me to come on, so I kicked off my satin evening slippers and tiptoed behind. According to the sign, the ship's fun deck—no old fogey shuffleboard allowed—had been closed for hours, but that didn't stop us."

"Please, skip to the wall. Did he climb it?"

"He took one look and backed away, but I was insistent and told him, 'You promised! You'll love it if you just give it a chance.' And besides, he might get over his fear of heights. Right after that I told him to hurry and get out of those clothes." Ruby snickered. "That's the very minute his whole attitude changed. He set the champagne bottle on a nearby table and ripped off his jacket and asked, 'Pants, too?' "

"Please, you can spare me those details."

"No, they are important. So, of course I insisted he strip down to his skivvies. Can you imagine him trying to navigate the wall in those polyesters?"

Ruby described reaching out to steady Lenny as he stepped out of his pink and blue plaid trousers. "I told him to stop worrying and that Bert climbs these all the time and he's about as graceful as a grizzly bear in a field full of butterflies. You know how Bert is, Andi."

"Yes, I know." That sleazy lawyer could stumble on a dust bunny. Still, that wasn't his worst trait. But don't get me started.

"Finally," Ruby continued, "he adjusted the waistband of his boxer shorts and sized up the ninety-degree incline to the summit of that silly fake mountain. When he started hemming and hawing, I knew I had to use my feminine wiles, so I walked my fingernails across his hairy back and whispered, 'You, my sweet, have what it takes. Just picture yourself shimmying right up that rock wall. Soon as you get harnessed in, that is.' He said something like 'what the hell' and opened the champagne. *Pop!* We turned toward the gate, scared late-night strollers might've overheard the uncorking ceremony. No one showed up, so he poured a glass of bubbly for me and one for himself...Oh, Andi, he gave the most beautiful toast. Let's see if I can get this right. He said, 'If I'm going to risk life and limb, might as well do it in style. To a special evening with a real jewel.' "

She drifted off to Ruby Land again, and I had to snap my fingers to bring her back.

"What? Oh, sorry. Guess I did it again. Anyway, when we clinked glasses, I remember adding, 'To killing off pesky old phobias.' "

I smothered a laughed at the irony of the toast and settled back in my chair. "Is that all you remember?"

"Is that all?" Giving me a blank stare, she looked skyward and tapped her cheek with her forefinger. "Nothing more than he climbed about fifteen feet before sliding down figuring it was more than enough to prove his manhood. He got dressed and walked me back to my cabin, gave me a kiss, and whispered in my ear."

She rolled her eyes and giggled.

Having no desire to hear intimate conversation, I changed the subject. "But according to the sheriff, an eyewitness account has you back to your cabin several hours later than you stated."

Her eyebrows furrowed. "An eyewitness account? Why, just ask Ethel. She knows when I got back. No, on second thought, she was snoring away at the time."

"Okay, okay." I'd heard enough. As to the muddled

timeline of Ruby's return, it was Ethel's word against hers. "If I may offer one suggestion, when you tell this story to the authorities, you might want to choose other descriptions besides *killing time* and *killing off pesky phobias.* No need to plant words or images in their heads that aren't there already."

I wasn't sure she understood my advice, but it was probably too little too late. After my meeting with the sheriff, I knew they had plenty of evidence connecting her to the crime.

In typical Ruby fashion, she changed moods— instantly. She bit her lower lip and whimpered, "Oh, if I hadn't goaded him into climbing that wall, he might still be alive. But I swear, Andi, he climbed down, got dressed, and walked me back to my cabin. The last time I saw him, he was living and breathing. Oh, my sweet Lenny."

My sweet Lenny? I remember back when she only had eyes for *my sweet Drew.* What did Dad ever see in her? She'd made a habit of being late—making grand entrances—from our very first meeting when she strolled into the restaurant, forty-five minutes late, telling a long tale about spilling an entire bottle of Purple Passion Cologne on her best orange satin dressing gown, nearly asphyxiating the cat, and chipping her rodeo red nail polish. Ruby was a full-on conversational rainbow. *Ah, good times.* Wish I'd been more accepting of her then. Instead, resentment grew over the years Ruby and Dad were married, making my defense of her now much more difficult.

I moved to the only grimy, wire-covered window to allow Ruby to finish her meltdown privately.

Chapter 6

Small, imported cars flew down the busy street in front of the jail, dodging pedestrians oblivious to any danger. Vendors crowded the sidewalks, peddling jewelry, pottery, magnificently colored blankets. Funny, I'm probably the only travel agent in the world who had never been to Cancun for fun. Oh, to have my restored cherry-red Mustang convertible here. I pictured driving to the beach in the evening, with a certain lawman in the passenger seat. Moonlight and mojitos. I could get into that.

"Hon? You all right?" Ruby's irritatingly nasal tone shattered my daydream, or night dream, depending on the scenario.

I turned away from the window and back to Ruby. "Yeah, I'm fine."

I was annoyed at being brought back to reality, but that didn't change the facts. Ruby's situation had no short-term solution. According to her, the last time she saw Lenny, he was alive. Who was telling the truth? Yep, I was definitely in for the long haul.

"Oh, by the way," I said, "Bert called. He's frantic with worry." I lied and sat back down across from her. "He's on his way, but I'm not sure whether he'll get here today or tomorrow."

"Oh, goody, goody!" Grief over her date's death dissipating, Ruby clapped her hands like a five-year-old spotting presents under the Christmas tree. "Bert will know what to do. Why, I'll bet he has me out of this nightmare of a place ten minutes after he gets here. Yes, Bert will know what to do."

I took no offense to Ruby's confidence in the shifty lawyer since she seemed to calm down at the mere mention of his name. *At least he's good for something.*

"Time's up," a tall, female deputy said from the opened door. "I mean now!"

"Oh, Andi Anna. Do I have to go back into that awful cell?" She leaned forward. "There are ladies of the night in there, and I'm afraid for my health. Who knows what kind of communicating diseases they have."

"Communicable, Ruby. And nothing is going to jump off them onto you." Not quite sure that was true, but I'd go with it, for the sake of Ruby's sanity and mine.

I loitered a moment too long from the deputy's perspective. She about split my eardrums, "Blondie! Do you not hear so good? Vamoose!"

I bit back a response and casually got to my feet, hoping to make a statement that I wasn't easy to push around. "Hang in there. I'll be back as soon as I can. Maybe with Bert."

I gave Ruby an uncharacteristic hug, despite the glare from the deputy, and strolled from the room.

After stepping from the visitation room, I finally could breathe easily. The place was clean, but it had a distinctive smell. Adding to my discomfort, I itched from head to toe. Probably my imagination working overtime from the detailed description of Ruby's cell and bunk mates. *My kingdom for a shower!* I fluffed my cotton blouse to get some air moving across my damp skin. Whew, I needed to scrub off the grime. How about getting a room, first? I pushed number one on speed dial.

"Graves Travel, Ellie speaking."

"Hey, El. It's me."

"Why, hey, Jonesy. How's it shakin' down there in Meh-hee-ko?"

Wonder if I'll ever get used to my travel assistant's twang? Hadn't happened in the three years she'd worked for me. Don't get me wrong. As slow as the travel agency business was these days, with most trips booked online by the vacationer, Ellie's gift of down-home gab had saved me from going under.

The contrast between Ellie's Southern twang and the rolled r's and fast-paced Spanish language, was striking. And I'd only been in Mexico for a few hours. It's doubtful I'd understand a word she said when I got back.

"Between the heat and Ruby's mess, it's awful down here, El. Worse than I ever imagined, but that's not why I'm calling."

"Oh, all *riiight*. What can I do ya for?"

Ellie did a lousy job masking disappointment. Well aware she thrived on gossip and gory details, I had neither time nor patience to gab on the phone for an hour just to satisfy her curiosity. I needed a decent place to crash—fast.

"Please book me a room, at least for the night. Well, better make that two nights. Close to the jail, if possible, but please, not like the dive you booked in Key West last month."

"You got it, Jonesy. Sorry about that Drunken

Parrot fiasco. Last time I'll listen to my friend, Lorna, I can tell you that. Anyhoo, I have the address of the police station and will look for something decent that's close by. I'll give ya a shout when I have the reservation. Bye."

Ellie's abrupt hang up left no doubt she was disappointed in the lack of juicy details, but I had faith she'd get right to work finding the best deal on the entire peninsula. Now, if she would just stop calling me Jonesy.

"Señorita Jones? Were you able to see your stepmother?" Manny walked out of his office just as I reached the door.

Hmmm. I knew there was a reason I took the non-direct exit route from the visitor's room. I did my best community theater performance and feigned surprise at seeing him.

"Oh, hello, Sheriff." I added a casual head-toss for good measure. "Yes, I visited Ruby, but a lot of good it did. Although something she said made me wonder if anyone investigated the woman who delivered the room service order that night."

He leaned against the doorframe, legs and arms crossed, fit for the cover of a romance novel. A steamy one, at that. "We checked her background but gathered very little information. I imagine she's working illegally, as is the case on some of the cruise ships that dock here. They have such turnover in the industry she could have boarded at the last port. Why do you ask?"

"During an honest-to-goodness lucid Ruby moment, she described getting bad vibes from the woman, and about their encounter. Plus, her story and your witness's story don't match." Given the skeptical look on the sheriff's face, I added, "I'm just wondering if your star witness to a murder deserves more scrutiny."

"*Un momento, por favor.*" Manny walked into his office and made a quick phone call. Returning, he announced, "It's done. A detective owes me a favor, so he's promised to see what he can dig up—quickly. Anything else you'd care to share from your visit?"

The image of Lenny's body hanging from the harness came to mind. "Can you tell me whether Lenny was dressed when the ship's security found him?"

Manny opened the folder and flipped through a couple of pages. "Yes. It says here he was fully dressed in slacks and sports coat. He was also wearing shoes and socks."

Different from Ruby's account. "Odd attire for climbing, don't you think?"

"Yes, that is strange." He closed the file and walked around the desk. "While we're waiting to hear back about information on the witness, would you care for some iced tea?"

"Made with local water and ice cubes?" I laughed. "What do you have against me?"

"No, no. At the Casa de Cancun restaurant located in an Americanized hotel just two blocks away." His forehead wrinkled like a boy wrongly accused of breaking a window with a baseball. "What do you take me for, señorita?"

"In that case, I accept your invitation." I wasn't convinced iced tea would be the most satisfying libation, but the company could—definitely—quench my thirst.

Chapter 7

Should have stuck to iced tea.

I made the mistake of trying to sit up, but the spinning room slammed me back onto the mattress.

"What the hell?" Did I get hit by a truck? Maybe if I just opened one eye. That worked. The room came into focus. Oh, yeah, it's the one Ellie booked for me. Was it yesterday afternoon, or had I been in vertigo hell for days? The bright patterned walls and drapes, which looked so cheery and tropical when I checked in, now prompted a gag response.

I grabbed for my watch—1:00 p.m. "What have I done to deserve this?"

I swear the evening started innocently in a lively but intimate cantina. "You still want iced tea," Manny had asked, "or would you prefer something a little bolder?"

My last coherent memory was leaping from iced tea straight to the hard stuff. Vague recollections flashed in between head throbs—sitting at the cantina bar, with a triple margarita on the rocks cradled in my hands. Yes, it was so big I had to use both hands. Oh, but I wasn't through.

At some point when Manny asked if I should really have another one, I recall throwing back my head and scoffing. "I can drink you under the table, my fine *federale.*"

"I'm local police, señorita, not federal." He'd humored me.

"I knoooow. I just like saying, fed-der-al-lee." I believe it was at that point in the evening I slid off the bar stool and leapt onstage.

The buzzing sound of a million mosquitoes filled the room, lasted a few seconds, and then stopped. Buzzed, again. My cell danced the *Merengue* on the nightstand.

Having no luck swatting at the annoying racket, I flipped it over and squinted. Bagley, Bert on the caller ID. Oh, swell. Could my morning get worse? Obviously. "Yeah, Bert?"

Two hours, four aspirin, and three cups of coffee later, I stood in front of the police station talking to the last person I'd want to be seen with in Cancun—or on the face of the Earth.

"Wow!" Bert said. "This place is something. Anything you can recommend, Miss Travel Agent Extraordinaire?"

"You're not here to sightsee, Bert." I gave a cursory glance at his bright yellow sport coat, white pants, white belt, and matching shoes. Straight out of the late '70s. I looked skyward and relished the image of a disco ball crashing onto his dreadful comb-over.

"Oh, sure, sure." He took a handkerchief out of his pants pocket and wiped beads of sweat from his forehead. "Whew, lordy, it's hot as blazes here. I could use an air-conditioned craps table right now. Since I can't spend every second with Ruby, I figured I'll slip away for an occasional game. Got a place in mind?"

"I'm no lawyer, Bert." *And you're not much of one.* "But these are serious charges. Not something that's going to be dropped the moment you vouch for Ruby's character. There are eyewitnesses and evidence pointing to her guilt."

I caught him rolling his eyes. "Now you just let me handle everything. In the meantime, be a good girl and hunt me up the best, most luxurious resort, with a first-class casino, of course." He stuffed the sweat-stained handkerchief back in his pocket and started through the door but thought better of it and stepped back. "After you, sugar."

I hated when he called me sugar, or good girl. I shoved Ellie's business card into his outstretched hand. "Call my assistant at the agency. Maybe she'll get your room, *sweetie*."

When we reached the sheriff's office, I sighed with relief and disappointment. He wasn't there.

"*El sheriff se ocupa del negocio personal*," a deputy doing filing said. "Personal business," he added for our benefit.

Just as well. I wasn't in the mood to introduce Bert, or face Manny. Having no memory how last evening ended—nor how I got back to my hotel room, into bed, and undressed—was nothing I wanted to face, especially in front of some deadbeat lawyer.

"'Scuse me, seen-yooore!" Bert yelled. I supposed he was compensating for his lack of Spanish comprehension. "I'm Missus Ruby Jones's attorney, Bert Bagley. I'm here to see my client."

"*Mis simpatías, Licenciado*." The deputy disappeared down the hallway, shaking his head.

"Huh? What'd he say? I don't know why they can't speak good ol' American English."

"Possibly because we're in Mexico, Bert. Could

you be any more offensive? My Spanish isn't that great, but I believe he extended his sympathies to you as Ruby's exalted lawyer. Apparently, she's been acting like, well, like Ruby."

"Oh, not good." Bert paced.

At least we agreed on something.

The deputy reappeared and motioned from the end of the hallway.

"We can see Ruby now. And, Bert, think back to when you were an honest-to-God, practicing attorney. Rumor has it you were pretty sharp. Suppose you can summon up a couple of first-rate legal ghosts?"

"No sweat, sugar. Watch the master."

Ruby jumped straight into his arms and squealed like a preteen at the latest boy band concert. "Oh, Bert. You're a sight for sore eyes. They've been treating me like a prisoner in this place. Please say you're getting me outta here."

"Good to see you, too, Ruby." Bert set her down and clutched his back. "Why don't we, uh, sit down? My dogs are killing me. Don't worry your pretty little head. I'm on it, but they're not going to release you on my say-so. I have your file, here, so give me a minute to get up to speed."

They sat down, and he pulled half-glasses from his breast pocket.

I couldn't believe my eyes. Bert actually looked and sounded like a lawyer. Who knew? I sat next to Ruby and distracted her while he studied the case. "How was your night?"

From her sour expression, not good. "My night? *My* night? Oh, it was perrrfect. Rosaria, she's my bunkmate, sang some Spanish song all night long. If I hear, 'Ay, ay, ay, ay' one more time, I'm gonna scream."

"You're such a song buff, I'm surprised you didn't belt out some show tunes yourself."

Before I could brace for a full half-hour rant, she smirked and changed the subject. "But enough about me. You don't look so good, hon."

I laughed nervously, my voice rising to embarrassing heights. "Strange bed, strange country. Trying to figure out how to get you out of this mess. Why should I look good?"

She gasped. "No need to get defensive. I was just making small talk."

With unusually perfect timing, Bert shut the case file and cleared his throat. "Got yourself in a pickle, huh, Ruby?"

Her red-rimmed eyes teared up. "Why won't anyone believe me? I didn't kill Lenny. In fact, I won't kill anything." She tapped my forearm. "Andi Anna, tell him how I coax daddy longlegs into tissues and shoo them gently out the back door. And I've had a family of geckos living with me for years."

"I can vouch for that." How many times had I seen little green and brown lizards running across Ruby's living room ceiling, down bright turquoise walls? "Your empathy toward bugs and reptiles, however, doesn't change facts. They have enough evidence to hold you."

"Which is exactly why I'm here," Bert interjected. "Now, as I see it…"

To my horror, he bit off the end of a big stogie.

"What? I'm not lighting it." He feigned indignation. "Is it okay if I just chew on it?"

He stuck the raw end of the disgusting cigar in his mouth and spun it around like a lumberjack in a logrolling contest.

"Now, the way I see it," he said, "this room service broad is our main problem. Do we know anything about her besides she may be from Nevada?"

Nevada? Wonder where he came up with that? "Manny—I mean Sheriff Gonzales is working on her identity through a detective-friend," I said.

"Manny, huh? You're on a first-name basis with the sheriff?" Bert smirked but rolled smoothly into his spiel about the case and what the next move should be.

I heard some mention of bail but couldn't erase thoughts of the previous night. I had a vague memory of being lifted off my feet and my head placed gently on a pillow. A noticeable shiver ran the full length of my spine.

"Right, Andi? Andi?"

"What!"

Bert reared back. "Whoa. What set you off? I was just telling Ruby, considering her clean record, I might be able to get bail as long as she stays in the country. That'll mean someone, oh say a next of kin, stays with her to guarantee she's not a flight risk."

Before I could spit out, no freaking way, Ruby shrieked, "Oh, it has to be you, Andi Anna! We'll have so much fun. Lounging on the beach, shopping in the markets, and the margaritas! I hear they're heavenly down here."

No, no. This can't happen! "Whoa, let's don't get ahead of ourselves. One, I have a job, remember? I can't run off for weeks and leave my business. Ellie needs help." No need to mention it was the exact opposite. From day one, I had been bewildered. Then a brash young platinum blonde, with far too much eye makeup, strolled in, plopped the Help Wanted sign on my desk, and announced, "I kin start, t'daaay." And she did. Ellie had surpassed expectation from that day on as My Girl Friday.

"And? Is there a number two, or are you just messing with me?"

"Oh, sorry. Just spaced out for a second. Anyway, two—and this is big, Ruby—you cannot, under any circumstances, go into a bar, let alone get skunk faced on margaritas." Trust me, I knew the consequences. Or did I?

"She's got a point there," Bert said. "That'll be part of your bail requirements. You must stay sober and under the radar."

Again, I was amazed. *Who are you, and what have you done with Bert?*

"Well, if nothing else, I'm going back to that ship and get my clothes." Ruby pulled at her orange prison jumpsuit and huffed. "Just look at this shapeless ol' thing. Orange does nothing for my complexion. Besides, I can't be seen in a tropical paradise without my new cruise wear. I bought turquoise sandals and jewelry, especially a gorgeous silver ankle bracelet, just for the trip. Why I'd be—"

"You'll go nowhere near that boat, Ruby," Bert said firmly. "Andi, do you think you could arrange to get her belongings? You do have an *in* with the law down here, don't you?" He winked.

My neck and cheeks flushed. "No, I don't have an *in* as you put it, but I'll see what I can do to get a couple of outfits for you, Ruby. Oh, and by the way, if you do get out on bail, you'll probably be given a special ankle bracelet." That reference went right over her head. Maybe Bert could explain it to her.

"And my makeup, Andi. Don't forget my makeup and hair combs." She made another vain attempt to straighten her hairpiece. "I must be a sight."

I studied her mascara-smeared eyelids and splotchy cheeks, murmured "thank you, Lord" that she had no apparent access to mirrors, and lied like a dog. "Considering all you've been through in the past twenty-four hours, you look terrific."

Bert chewed on his soggy cigar.

"I'll do what I can to get on the ship," I said. "May not be easy since I'll have to first get to Playa del Carmen and catch a ferry to the port in Cozumel." That, alone, would be an all-day process. "Maybe the Sheriff's Department can help with the transportation."

Bert smirked. "Oh, I'm sure it can. Anything for the head guy's Miami sweetie."

With more effort than I cared to admit, I brushed off the middle school humor. "I'll let you know before I go, Ruby. Make a list."

Ruby stamped her foot. "I still don't see why I can't go with you. Not that I don't appreciate your offer, but you'll probably forget something if I'm not with you." She paused for a moment and shouted, "Oh, oh, I know! Ask the twins to help you. Doris and Cloris. They're in the cabin right across from me."

Hmm. Interesting she didn't mention her roomie. "You don't think Ethel could help?"

Ruby stuttered. "I—I'm sure she could, but don't bother her. Cloris and Doris will know what I need."

Something in her voice hit me wrong. Ethel was

her best friend. I wondered what happened between them that would make her skittish about asking her to help gather clothing and personal items. More to the point, I wondered what happened to encourage Ethel to report such damning evidence against Ruby. I made a mental note to grill the twins. "Okay, I'll leave her out of it, but first I have to find out if I can even get on the ship."

Ruby folded her arms and pouted. "What's the use of getting out at all if you can't even promise to get my stuff? I might as well stay in jail for all you care."

"Suit yourself." I strolled to the door. "See ya sometime next year, when your trial begins."

"No, wait! Oh, Andi Anna, don't you know a joke when you hear one? Cross my heart and hope to die. No, wait—" She laughed and clapped a hand over her mouth. "Let me try this again. You two get me outta here, and I'll be the best girl ever."

She cozied up to Bert.

Yeah, and I have a winning lottery ticket in my pocket.

I closed door and she shouted, "I'll make a list for you!"

"Sure you will," I muttered. *How about I make a list of all your annoying habits?* Dad had married her more than six years ago, and she'd been barking orders and getting her way ever since. Ruby specialized in manipulation. No sense wasting energy when she could coerce others into doing her bidding.

We were like oil and water from the very beginning, despite my half-hearted efforts to accept her. So why should I stay in Mexico to fight for her freedom? With one phone call to Ellie, I could get a plane ticket home and live without the constant interference and annoyance that shadowed Ruby like a churning thundercloud. Easy decision, huh? Not so much. What I couldn't live with was the inevitable guilt from letting down Dad.

With that settled, I needed a plan. Walking onto a cruise ship and expecting clues to fall in my lap was not a plan.

Let's see. First I'd need to look for anyone involved with ship security that may have information about the murder and those involved. They might be willing to steer me to the woman who delivered the late-night meal to Lenny's cabin. Ruby had a bad feeling about her. Next, I'd hunt down Ruby's friends, starting with Ethel, if possible.

Chapter 8

Relief poured over me. Ruby was no longer my total responsibility, and I left Bert to plot his next legal move. All I had to do was somehow get to the cruise ship, gather enough clothes, makeup, and accessories to get stepmommy off my back, and get about a million questions answered.

I proceeded toward the police station exit muttering, "Let her sob black mascara-laced tears on Bert's cheesy yellow sport coat for a while. I'll be free to check out other leads."

"Excuse me?" Manny loomed in the hallway, a bemused smile on his face.

"Oh, Sheriff Gonzales. I, uh…" Don't stutter. Don't blush. Whatever you do don't blush. "I was just leaving."

He leaned against the doorframe, his arms folded across his broad chest. "Not without saying goodbye, I hope."

Darn! I pictured my cheeks turning the putrid shade of cranberry highlights my *former* colorist slapped on my hair last year. Worse, my attempt at a sexy laugh sounded more like a bullfrog serenading his lady friend. "I wasn't sure you were still here, but, since you are, I have a request."

"In that case, I'm glad I didn't miss you. Please come in."

He paused before walking into his office. "By the way, how did your visit go? Did your ex-stepmother cause you any problems?"

Relieved to talk about the case, instead of, well, you know...I answered, "Oh, no, nothing I didn't expect. In fact, she was able to fill in some of the details for her lawyer, Mr. Bagley."

"Speaking of that—" He took a file off his desk. "—I received a preliminary report on the woman who delivered the room service order to Señor La Mour's cabin. There's not much information, I'm afraid, other than she's listed on the ship's employment records as Carmelita Vasquez, originally from Nevada."

"Hmm. Ruby's lawyer also mentioned Nevada as her last known residence. This may be coincidental, but according to Ruby, Lenny La Mour, in his younger days, was a huge star in Las Vegas."

"It's probably just coincidence, since cruises hire many semi-retired entertainers, but, just in case, my detective friend is searching the city for the last known address of Ms. Vasquez."

"The city? Las Vegas? Did she work there, too?"

"She did, but that's where my friend hit a dead end. It's as if five years ago she fell off the face of the Earth."

Hmm. Ruby's suspicions of the woman who delivered their room order might be valid. I found it hard to believe anyone could just disappear in this age of cell phone cameras and social media. "Did he search online? What about the FBI database? And the casinos? They have surveillance videos and keep very detailed photographic records of all employees."

Manny sighed, patiently. "My friend is an

experienced detective. Don't you suppose he's tried all you're suggesting?"

Don't look into his eyes, Andi. Stay away from the eyes. There was too much at stake. "I'm sure your friend is highly qualified, but even the best detective could miss something. Uh, could you hold on a moment?"

I dug out my cell and phoned Ellie. "Hey, El—huh? Oh, yeah, sure. I'll hold." *Guess I can't complain she doesn't consider her boss's call a priority. She is busy with customers.* "Yeah, I'm still here. No, please, Ellie. I need to talk to—"

Click.

I shrugged off impatience and embarrassment. "My assistant. She's…taking care of an important client and will call back. In the meantime, I'm considering going to Las Vegas."

Funny how that idea just popped in my head. Was I hoping to avoid facing possible indiscretions? No!

I continued, "This new information about the main witness having lived in Vegas is worth checking. I'm not willing to accept a dead end."

The easy smile left Manny's face. "Do you think that's wise, Señorita Jones?"

"Don't you think, after last night, you can call me Andi?"

Was that a twinkle in his eye?

"As a gentleman, I would never mention it. But since you brought it up, where did you learn to dance like that? On the bar, no less."

"I danced on the bar? Really? I'm a terrible dancer. My sister has to drag me onto the dance floor, and even then."

The corners of his mouth twitched. "I'm kidding. I have no knowledge of your dancing ability, on the floor or the bar." He raised one very sexy eyebrow. "But I do know you're a bit gullible. No, you didn't dance, but you did sing with the band, or tried to. They humored your attempt to join them during 'La Cucaracha' because you were having such a great time. Your inhibitions appeared to diminish with every ounce of tequila consumed, despite my best efforts to get you to stick to nonalcoholic beverages."

"How did I—uh, I mean, who took me back to my room?" I tugged at my collar, hoping to release some of the heat rising up my chest.

"I did. More like, half carried, half dragged you back to your room. I hope you don't mind that I searched your handbag for a hotel key card. It's fortunate you were able to mumble where you were staying, otherwise I would've had a very long and frustrating search through the myriad of tourist hotels."

I still hadn't gotten the answer to the most important question, but did I really want to go there? *Face it, Andi. You have to know.* "I assume, then, you were the one who…put me to bed."

He bowed. "It was my pleasure."

I'm certain the tone of my cheeks passed cranberry and headed toward deep scarlet.

"But before you get the wrong idea, I averted my gaze when I undressed you and left as soon as you fell asleep."

"You mean, when I passed out?"

"I can tell the difference through training and experience. The fact you had a tiny smile on your face, and snored, softly, made it clear you had fallen asleep quite naturally." He raised those perfect eyebrows again and added, "Oh, and no need to thank me for hanging your dress in the closet. I just assumed you didn't want to sleep in it, or leave it crumpled on the floor."

My mind whirled. *Had I been wearing my granny panties?*

No, thank heavens. I woke up the next morning in the black slinky lingerie set that Ruby—imagine the irony—got me last Christmas when she said, "You don't want to go around in those big ol' bloomers, Andi. You just never know." *Guess I owe you another one, Ruby.*

My phone vibrated in my pocket. *Ah-ha! Saved by the cell.* "Hi, El. Yeah, that's okay. Hang on a minute." I'd give her a little of her own medicine. "I need to get my assistant moving on plane and hotel reservations, Sheriff, but first, can you arrange to get me on the ship before it leaves port so I can gather Ruby's belongings?"

"Let me make a phone call to see what is being held in evidence."

"Fine." I stuffed my cell back in my bag, and a high-pitched twang echoed from my phone. "Jonesy? Hey, Jonesy. You there? I got four lines on hold."

I pulled my phone back out and slapped it to my ear. "Sorry, El. Okay, ready? I need a flight out of here, ASAP, to Las Vegas. Huh? No!"

I mouthed "just a minute" to Manny and walked swiftly out of his office, down the hallway, and out of earshot.

"I haven't met anyone." I would not give Ellie that kind of ammunition. She'd never give me a moment's peace until I described every inch of Manuel Gonzales.

After that, she'd need pictures. "Are you working on that flight? Okay, text as soon as you can. I have one stop to make, but if all goes as planned, I should be able to get out of here late tomorrow morning."

Manny walked from his office. "The ship is leaving for Aruba tomorrow morning. If you can get there today, you'll have one hour to gather clothes for Señora Jones."

"That's not a lot of time. I don't want to accidently remove evidence. How will I know what I can take?"

"All that's of any use in the case has already been analyzed or removed, so you should have no problem, but one hour on board was all I could get you."

"Thanks. I can't imagine telling Ruby she'd have to spend one more day in that orange prison jumpsuit, if her lawyer gets her released that is." I stopped short of grilling Manny about that possibility. "Oh, and who should I ask for?"

"Here's the phone number. The head of security is waiting for your call and will arrange for someone to meet you at the gangplank. You'll need to get to Playa del Carmen as soon as possible. There, a ferry will take you to the port. Just remember, you got—"

"I know, I know. One hour."

"And please, Señorita Jones, do not fly to Las Vegas without talking to me first. I consider it a terrible idea." He grabbed a card from his desk drawer. "My personal cell number is listed. Please call, day or night."

I nodded and took the card but had no need for his approval. Despite the unfortunate events of the previous night, I needed him to believe I could take care of myself. I wished I felt as confident.

I hailed a cab to Playa del Carmen, about a half-hour south, with favorable traffic. Settling back, I tried to relax while the cabbie swerved to avoid traffic and pedestrians. Guess it would've been nice if Manny had offered to let me hitch a ride on one of their police boats. I wasn't going to ask, especially after I brushed off his warning about flying to Vegas.

And what was the deal in reminding me over and over that I had one hour. One hour. I could easily be on and off that ship in a flash if I wanted. But since the plan was to snoop around while I was there, two or three hours sounded realistic. My watch said 2:00 p.m. If travel-agent memory served me right, I'd be on board by 4:00 p.m. for high tea. Last evening's hangover was a thing of the past, and my stomach was rumbling. After a quick pass through the buffet line, I'd get lost among the passengers for some evidence gathering of my own.

Grilling Ethel and the twins was priority one.

Chapter 9

The half hour cab ride took more than an hour. We made it to the dock with five minutes to spare before the ferry departed. "This doesn't look too bad."

A double-deck ferry, filled with passengers, drifted benignly while preparing to set out across the narrow strip of Caribbean water between the mainland and Cozumel. I'd fought off seasickness listening to client horror stories about crossing from the mainland to the island. Waves could get quite high, threatening to capsize small boats. I scanned the bay. Smooth seas. I was glad I nixed those seasickness pills. Even the nondrowsy kind made me groggy. Considering my limited amount of time on the ship, I had to stay alert.

By the time I boarded, passengers—umbrella festooned drinks in hand—were well into the party atmosphere. Music blared, and couples in flowered tourist shirts and straw hats danced around the deck with no concept of rhythm or coordination. A few women wore tropical sundresses. Others skipped excessive clothing and went straight to bikinis. More than a few should've reconsidered that decision. On the other hand, who was I to judge after my own embarrassing performance with the mariachi band?

Settling on a comfy padded bench in the middle, one of the few left, I ignored the commotion and made mental notes about what I wanted—needed—to accomplish.

The first order of business: get Ruby's gear. With Bert's help, I'm sure, she texted a very specific list: pink capris with a green, pink, and turquoise blouse. White capris with blue- and white-striped nautical T-Shirt. The scooped neck not the V neck! Turquoise shorts (knee-length) with three white tops (parrot emblem, purple trim, green-stripes). All makeup, accessories, five scarves, jewelry, and hair products. The text ended in bold letters: Don't forget to pack hairspray, hair clips, and all three brushes.

I closed the message and shoved the phone in my bag. *You'll get whatever I can stuff into that suitcase, Ruby. Geesh.* How could one woman deliver that much aggravation?

Our full ferry of vacationers left the dock a few minutes late, although the captain assured over the loudspeaker we were right on schedule and would arrive at precisely 3:45 p.m. Goody! I'd be in time for the afternoon buffet. Years of experience, with my fussy blood sugar levels, affirmed I'd be unable to concentrate on an empty stomach. So, for Ruby's sake, I'd need a pastry, or two, before serious sleuthing commenced.

Ten minutes into the trip, live music played, and alcohol flowed even more freely, if that was possible. I passed on a piña colada, for obvious reasons. I'd leave drunken dancing to the sun-burned vacationers from Wisconsin. A two-man, one-woman group played guitar, tambourine, and flute. Ever hear "La Bamba" on flute? Trust me, you haven't missed anything.

Much as I vowed to concentrate on the task ahead, the deep azure water beckoned. Try as I might, I had no memory, in my entire life, seeing that particular shade of blue. The sea captivated and hypnotized. Clinging to the rail, I envisioned being sucked into a maritime portal and spending the rest of my life with the sun and wind on my face.

"Attention, vacationers and partiers. We'll dock in five minutes. Please gather your personal belongings, grab another drink, and enjoy your time in Cozumel."

My daydream would have to wait. Reality called. No wormhole. No time warp. Rats! "It's show time."

My luck, Ruby's ship, one of three, was docked the farthest from the ferry port. I walked and walked and walked. The sun beat down. I uttered a few choice curse words because I hadn't bought one of those straw hats for sale at the port.

Arriving at the gangplank—tired, hungry, grumpy, on the verge of heat stroke—a woman in an immaculately pressed white uniform yelled from above. "Miss Jones?"

I shielded my eyes from the afternoon sun.

"Please, come to the top deck," she said.

I guessed satisfying my hunger would have to wait. I trudged up ten sets of stairs. For once in my life, I longed for an elevator.

"I'm Helena Morrison, head of security. Goodness, you're sweating. Did you walk up? The elevator was inside on your left."

Now she tells me. "I needed the exercise, anyway. Hi, Ms. Morrison, I'm Andi Jones," I huffed and puffed. "Did we talk on the phone earlier?"

"No, you spoke to my assistant."

"How did you recognize me way down there? I don't remember describing myself."

"High-tech, Miss Jones. We were emailed a copy of your driver's license. Plus, I have these." She smiled and held out a pair of mini binoculars. "Everyone who comes on board is thoroughly scrutinized."

Not thoroughly enough, I wanted to say. Someone on this ship got away with murder.

"So, if you're ready, I'm here to escort you to the cabin you wish to see. Gathering items for one of the passengers, I'm told."

I took an instant liking to this pleasant, self-assured woman. She barely came to my shoulder, yet I determined from her handshake, she was one tough cookie. I'd bet former military. She removed her hat, revealing deep auburn hair gathered in a stylish French braid. A pair of gray-tinted sunglasses completed the outfit.

"Please, follow me."

She did say, please, but I recognized an order, not a request. We walked down three flights of steps to one of the dark, narrow hallways triggering my never-fail claustrophobia. In case I was truly limited to one hour, I decided to subtly pump her for information. "So, you had quite a disturbance the other night, huh? Bet you don't find too many dead passengers hanging from walls."

She peered over the top of her glasses. "I'm sorry, Miss Jones. I'm not at liberty to discuss the incident, especially since your stepmother is involved in the investigation."

Something in her voice left the impression she resented my appearance on Ruby's behalf. Maybe I wasn't going to like Miss Snooty Morrison so much after all.

We walked in silence to a door covered with yellow crime tape at the end of the hall.

"This was Ms. Jones's cabin. Her roommate, Ms. Lipton, has been assigned another since the investigation is ongoing, but her new room isn't ready yet. I believe she's on the sundeck having tea if you'd like to see her."

Ethel. I'd been so caught up in Ruby's drama I hadn't considered the effect on her friend and cabinmate. "Is Ethel—Ms. Lipton—okay?"

"She was, quite naturally, shaken up over the tragic events. But before she left, she gathered your stepmother's clothes and belongings that weren't part of the evidence."

"That was kind of her."

Ms. Morrison removed her sunglasses and pulled back the crime tape. "I'll be right outside the door, and remember, you must be off the ship in—"

"Yes, I know. One hour."

I stepped inside, closed the door in her face and turned to the task at hand, fighting the impulse to run back into the hallway. Even with fake window curtains, inside cabins were a claustrophobe's worst nightmare. Next time I needed to get Ruby an upgrade. *If there is a next time.*

The tight space was only half the problem. Ruby's clothes and personal items were strewn in an unorganized heap on the bed next to the wall. Looking for something in your friend's personal items, Ethel? My suspicions had no real basis, other than gut instinct. According to dear stepmom, every one of her friends was jealous of her attractiveness to eligible men. So, why pick on Ethel?

No time to match outfits, I hurriedly stuffed makeup, hair paraphernalia, and as many clothes as I could fit in Ruby's red, lady-bug festooned suitcase she'd bragged about the weekend before the cruise. She had relished in the belief that Ethel and the twins were going to be so envious since they had to tie colored yarn around their old black suitcases to keep them straight from the rest of the tacky luggage. Besides, she had said, ladybugs were good luck.

How's that luck working for ya, Ruby?

I jumped at the knock on the door. "Miss Jones? How are you doing?"

"Fine, Ms. Morrison." I peeked out. "I'll be there in a minute."

"You have time left, but there are other security matters that need my attention, so I'd appreciate wrapping this up as quickly as possible."

How am I going to lose her? Other security matters, maybe? Perhaps I could add to her workload. I stepped into the head, shut the door, and called the ship's phone number Manny supplied at the station. "Yes, security? I'm on the D-Deck walkway, and I just saw a large object fall from what appears to be the pool deck. Please send someone immediately. A passenger may have fallen! Hurry!"

I listened at the door. Sure enough, a phone rang.

"Morrison. Yes, I'm still here with Miss Jones. But let me check it out. In the meantime, send Hugo down here."

"Miss Jones?"

"I just have a few more of Ruby's things to gather."

"Unfortunately, I have to go, but one of my

assistants is on the way to escort you off the ship. Please wait for him."

"Sure will." *Sure won't!* By the time they figured out the emergency was bogus, I'd be on my way to find Ethel and the twins.

I shut Ruby's suitcase and eased open the door, taking a quick glance down the hallway. No sign of Ms. Morrison or her replacement. *Okay, let's test your amateur sleuthing skills.* I rooted around in my purse for a piece of gum, removed the wrapper and chewed furiously. Spitting the softened gum into my fingers, I positioned it on the door frame before carefully closing the door. As planned, the gum not only kept the door from locking, but the small and undetectable crack it created guaranteed easy access should I need to get back in.

"Andi? Is that you?"

I practically jumped out of my sandals. One of Ruby's cruisemates poked her head out from the cabin across the hall. "Oh hi, Doris. You scared me half to death."

"I suppose, considering what Ruby's been through, that's fitting." She snickered at her joke. "Oh, I'm sorry, dearie. That was in poor taste. How is she doing? Is that her suitcase?"

Doris was a huge gossip, and I needed to talk to her, but if the security officer showed up and saw me loitering, I'd be escorted off the ship. "Uh, yeah. I gathered some clothes and personal items. You know how Ruby is about her appearance. Say, do you mind if I ask you a couple of questions?" Nothing like turning the tables on a snoop.

"Sure. Ask away."

"Not here in the hallway. Why don't we go into your cabin?"

Doris held the door as I slipped inside.

"Would you like to leave it open?" she asked. "Some people get claustrophobic in these closet-size rooms."

"Oh no," I lied. "I love tiny spaces. They're so— cozy." I shut the door and casually flipped the lock while her back was turned. "Where's your sister?"

"Oh, Cloris is flitting around here somewhere. She's probably first in line for afternoon tea. You know how she is about her sweets. If she can't nibble on something every two hours or so, she gets snappy."

My stomach rumbled on cue. "I know the feeling."

Doris motioned toward the tiny table and chairs in the corner. "Sit down and make yourself comfy. I want to hear all about poor Ruby's ordeal."

I'll just bet you do. I pulled out a chair, and Doris sat on the twin bed across from me. Muffled taps and a one-way conversation filtered from the hallway.

"Miss? Are you in there? I'm here to escort you off the ship."

"Is that for you?" Doris started to get up, but I shushed her with my raised index finger. She gave me a puzzled look but kept quiet until we heard retreating footsteps. "You're not hiding, are you?"

"No, of course not." I scrambled to change the subject. "I'm not sure how long they'll let me stay on board. Don't you want to hear all about Ruby?"

Doris nodded enthusiastically as I knew she would.

"Tell you what. I'll leave the suitcase here, and we'll go find Cloris. I'd love some tea and pastries."

"That's a wonderful idea." She sprang from the bed

and grabbed her straw beach bag. "You can fill in both of us at the same time, and that way I won't have to worry about leaving anything out when I give Sissy the scoop."

Like playing a fiddle. I was quite certain Doris and Cloris would put gossip above all else.

"Well, then what are we waiting for?" I edged toward the door. "Just in case that annoying security guard is lurking around, you check the hallway to be sure it's empty." A glance in the full-length mirror gave me another idea. "You wouldn't happen to have a hat and sunglasses I could borrow, would you? The sun is brutal down here, and my freckles are producing freckles."

Doris nodded. "I have the perfect hat. Wide-brimmed to protect your skin. I bought it especially for the cruise since I have the same problem with my complexion."

No, your freckles are age spots.

Don't be mean, Andi. Your day is coming.

Yes, mother.

"Here's the hat, and I found this adorable smock to cover your arms. You can't be too careful."

I gratefully accepted the turquoise beach hat, sequined cats-eye shades, and purple cover-up, carefully avoiding a second look in the mirror. No sense confirming how ridiculous I looked. The embarrassing fashion statement would be well worth any information I uncovered to help clear Ruby.

The twins, Ruby, and Ethel met years ago at a singles dance, long before Dad and Ruby were married. According to Cloris and Doris, they became instant friends. "Ruby was always thrilled to see us," Cloris would say, "especially when Ethel was there. The four of us were inseparable at every social event."

At the time, I had my suspicions about Ruby's motives. Then it dawned on me. As long as Cloris, Doris, and Ethel were hanging around, Ruby would shine in the looks department. Even though she was, usually, the most attractive woman in her age group, she methodically avoided competition. Hanging with Ethel and the twins guaranteed she'd be the belle of the ball.

I had no right to throw stones, however. I was well aware the sisters were about four sandwiches short of a picnic for six, yet there I was, having no problem taking advantage of their trusting nature. I felt a tad bit of guilt, but not for long. Now I only had to persuade a few others to talk. There had to be other witnesses who saw or heard something useful that involved a suspect other than Ruby.

I followed Doris up the stairs, confident I wouldn't be recognized. Ha!

Chapter 10

I swear the high tea buffet tables groaned beneath the weight of cookies, cakes, and muffins. Before digging in, I smirked at the security commotion on the opposite side of the pool deck. Ms. Morrison appeared appropriately occupied. Most likely, she and her associates were busy interviewing sunbathers about a possible passenger incident, thanks to yours truly. Not much chance I'd be spotted. Still, I pulled my hat down a little lower.

Doris snuck up on her sister who sat parked—and I do mean parked—at one of the fifty or so guest tables and whispered in her ear.

Cloris jumped, her hand flipping a loaded dessert plate upside down. What a waste! Chocolate mousse, red velvet cake, and vanilla crème puffs smashed into a gloopy, unrecognizable pile of flour, sugar, and cream. Prepared to give her sister a good tongue-lashing for destroying her afternoon gorge-fest, she spotted me. "Andi! As I live and breathe. Where did you come from?"

Doris shoved her sister back in the chair and yelled, "Are you deaf? What did I just tell you?"

Cloris leapt to her feet, hands on hips. "You told me not to yell, but now you're yelling so why can't I? Besides, you should've warned me Andi was here."

Doris got nose to nose with her sister. "I swear,

Cloris, you don't have the sense God gave a goose!"

Despite my best laid plans, passengers in both buffet lines, along with a dozen or so wait staff, stared. So much for anonymity.

"Uh, ladies," I whispered. "Please, let's lower the volume and sit down." I glanced across the atrium to the other side of the ship. Morrison and her posse were still occupied. No sign they'd heard our ruckus.

Cloris plopped glumly in her chair, still smarting from her sister's reprimand. The moment I sat, she smiled and whispered at the same volume most people talk normally, "I can't believe it's you, Andi. Oh, you must be here to see Ruby. Wait, you can't be here to see Ruby." Her eyes bulged, and her mouth flew open. She turned to her twin. "Oh, Doris, did anyone tell her about Ruby?"

Doris sighed. "Of course she knows about Ruby. Why do you think she's here?"

"Well, I don't know. How could I?"

"Because—"

"I'll explain everything, Cloris." I interrupted before their voices escalated again. "Let's just sit here quietly for a moment until everyone goes back to filling plates and enjoying the warm air and sunshine."

If security came over to check the noise level, I was dead.

"There, there, dear, I'm sure you're worried, but you must try these little cucumber sandwiches. At least *they* survived your assault!" Cloris gave her twin the stink-eye and patted the back of my hand. "Cucumbers are very good for you. You can use them for anything from shrinking puffiness under your eyes to getting rid of nasty grubs in your garden. Just imagine!"

I shifted, uncomfortably, at the thought of grubs squirming under my eyelids.

Doris huffed. "Cloris, if you'll shut your pie hole for one minute, Andi wants to fill us in on Ruby's predicament."

Cloris stuffed a bite-sized sandwich in her mouth and chewed fiercely. "I'm all ears," she squealed, oblivious to bits of bread and cucumber rind spewing from her mouth.

I looked from one twin to another. Doris, tall and gangly with wiry salt-and-pepper locks. Cloris, short and rotund with a blonde-from-a-bottle sixties coiffure. If Ruby said it once, she said it a million times, she wouldn't be one bit surprised if that mama of theirs was with two men nine months before they were born. It didn't matter that I had explained the difference between identical and fraternal.

I couldn't care less about their parentage but had to admit those two were a strange pair. The Dobsons would never be mistaken for sisters, let alone twins, but despite their obvious physical differences, they still dressed alike. Remind me never to step foot in the store that accommodates both taste and size options for Cloris and Doris.

"So?" Doris persisted. "Spill it!"

I calculated how much to reveal, settling on a path with just enough juicy tidbits to satisfy their curiosity and make them vulnerable to a couple of probing questions. "You know, Ruby's lawyer-friend, Bert, don't you?"

Doris blushed. "Oh my, yes. We see him on TV every day warning people about shady insurance companies out to cheat you if you have an accident."

I'd seen his deceptive commercials when I couldn't change the station fast enough.

Cloris nodded. "Oh yes, I love him. Is he going to help Ruby?"

I surrendered to the Bert Bagley Fan Club. "I hope so. He arrived today and has things rolling. First, he'll try to get bail set since Ruby has no previous record. Still, she's charged with murder, so he may not be successful."

I tiptoed through the story, and their undivided attention was broken only by a gasp or a "oh, my." I had about reached the limit of how much to say without compromising the evidence when my stomach demanded attention. "Are those blueberry scones on that lady's plate?"

"Oh yes," Cloris gasped. "I'll go with you since my first plate was destroyed."

Doris rolled her eyes. "I'll stay here until you two get back. Wouldn't want someone stealing our table before Andi has a chance to spill all the gory details."

I jumped up, eager to check out the goodies. Wonder how much more detail the sisters would need before we moved past Ruby and the mess she was in? I needn't have worried. The moment we returned, Doris was distracted and scrutinized every item on her sister's plate. "What's with the cookies? You hate oatmeal! You know parfait is ninety percent sugar, right? Don't come crying to me when you gain another ten pounds!"

I couldn't've planned it better. Mission accomplished. With Ruby on the back burner, I'd have a chance to quiz them about other participants in the unfortunate event. I leaned in at the same time as Cloris, leaving us nose to nose. Before I could ask my first question, she beat me to it. "Have you talked to Ethel?"

I pulled back far enough to focus—and avoid a heavy dose of cucumber breath. "Haven't seen her. Why?"

"Well, I spotted her, two days ago, passing along one of Ruby's hankies to a cabin boy. When I questioned her about it, she clammed up. Said I was seeing things. But I wasn't. The bright red embroidery with Ruby's name was plain to see as the nose on your face. She'd carried one of those hankies around ever since Drew died."

"That's right," Doris said, nodding repeatedly. "She always managed to tell us how they were specially made for her the first Christmas they were married. She did love him, you know?"

I cringed a bit. Yeah, I knew, deep down, she did. And he was devoted to her. Why couldn't I see the good in her? Dad did. Georgia did. Cloris and Doris did. I promised myself to do better, but first, I had to get Ruby's flaky butt out of jail.

I slumped back in my chair and processed Ethel's apparent betrayal. Sure, I'd had my suspicions about her, but without evidence, I'd considered them baseless.

Until now.

Was one of Ruby's oldest friends trying to frame her? "Why do you suppose Ethel would do that? You don't believe it's connected to the murder, do you?"

"Oh, we don't think that. However—" It was Doris's turn to lean forward, eyes narrowing into suspicious slits. "—Ethel has always been a loyal friend to us. But the whole incident was curious, especially when she fiercely denied it."

Cloris chimed in. "She'd been a little standoffish to Ruby, even before the cruise."

She clammed up, but I could tell by her body language she was on pins and needles waiting for me to ask.

"Why was that?"

Cloris's face lit up. "Well, you see, Ruby made fun of Ethel in front of a fella she was trying to impress."

"I remember that," Doris clucked. "The last senior holiday dance. Something about the way Ethel was dressed. I think Ruby's exact words were 'If you're going to wear spandex Capris, you really should find a good girdle to restrain that sack of potatoes bouncing behind you.' Ethel was mortified, especially since she struggles getting any man interested in her. Poor thing."

Cloris nodded sympathetically. "Harry. I believe his name was Harry."

"Well, Ethel turned all shades of red and Harry made some lame excuse and left. Soon as he was out of sight, Ethel lit into Ruby like a windmill in a tornado."

I shook my head. No wonder Ruby was hesitant to talk about her cabinmate. I wondered why she agreed to go on the birthday cruise at all. "Can't say I blame her. What about Lenny La Mour? Do you know anything about him, other than Ruby was quite infatuated?"

Doris rolled her eyes. "Oh, my. They were both putting on quite a show."

Cloris clapped her hand across her mouth and giggled. "Their hands were all over each other at the table. They were even more brazen on the dance floor!"

I held up my palm. "I get the picture. So, they were getting along? No harsh words or arguments?"

Cloris looked at Doris and shrugged.

Doris answered, "No, not that I saw.

"They seemed all lovey-dovey to me," Cloris added.

"So, a witness reported Ruby had bullied Lenny about his phobia of heights. Did it happen, or not?"

The twins account contradicted the "star" witness. They also provided another clue since neither could've known about Ruby's handkerchief being a crucial piece of evidence against her. Cloris and Doris had unwittingly set my next course of action: Confront Ethel before I was booted off the ship.

Ms. Morrison finally moved on. Leaping from my chair, I made my apologies. "Sorry, ladies. Duty calls."

Doris's eyes widened. "Are you going to give Ethel the third degree?"

"Oh, can we come along?" Cloris clapped her hands in delight.

I sprinted to the buffet table, grabbed a napkin and a cherry something-or-other, and called over my shoulder, "Gotta run! You two stay and enjoy the rest of the afternoon. I'll keep you posted."

"But what about my things, Andi Anna?"

I paused wondering what *things* Doris referred to. Then I remembered. How could I forget those gaudy accessories? "I'll get them back to you before I leave."

Despite the sour expressions of disappointment on their faces as I made my getaway, I was satisfied with the first piece of the puzzle. Ethel, and her possible tampering with evidence, opened a whole new avenue into Lenny's death. *Now, to find the old battle axe, Ruby's dear friend.*

I weighed the option of getting Manny's opinion on this new information but knew he'd tell me to let the

Mary Cunningham

professionals handle it. Well, I am a professional. Okay, so I'm a professional travel agent, not a detective, but my determination to get Ethel to talk one way or the other, centered on getting to the truth.

Fairly certain Ms. Morrison and her gang were still occupied by my fake, call-in accident scene, I headed back to D-deck in case Ethel had returned to the cabin. No one in sight, which confirmed my suspicion that all cruise passengers ever did was eat and sleep. Oh, and gamble, although I couldn't picture Ethel at the slots.

Good! My gum trick worked. The door popped open. I picked the sticky wad off the hallway carpet so no one would step on it, especially me. No sign of life inside. Now, where would a senior citizen be at 4:30 in the afternoon if not at the buffet? Had she arrived after I left? Not possible. The gum was intact when I got there.

I picked up a brochure from the table next to Ethel's bed. *High-Seas Spa and Beauty Salon.* The time, 1:30 p.m., was scrawled at the top of the flyer. Inside, a list of services suggested the full treatment would be an all-day process. If Ethel had an afternoon appointment, chances were good she was still there.

"God bless the spa that makes you beautiful, Ethel."

Chapter 11

Spotting the stairs to the main deck, I could bypass the elevator. If I'd made ten flights without keeling over, four should be a breeze.

Bright lights, stores on both sides, and salespeople dressed to the hilt and brandishing plastered smiles waited to—*ahem*—relieve passengers of their vacation cash. High-end perfume lined the shelves of one small shop. Floral and musk permeated the air. Whiffs of essential oils, varying from eucalyptus to citrus to herb, confused and overpowered my nasal passages.

I slipped quickly into a jewelry and watch shop. Glints of shiny gold and sparkling diamonds drew me to large display cases. No need for more jewelry, but I was looking for a new sports watch that tracked steps, heartbeat, sleep patterns, etc. The one I'd had for three years conked out more than a month ago. Besides, showing an interest in a purchase might make the store owner receptive to answering a couple of questions.

A distinguished-looking older gentleman glanced—briefly, his nose higher than necessary—when I entered the store.

"Excuse me. Do you have any smart watches?"

Peering over tortoiseshell half glasses, he gave me the once-over. The disdainful expression made it clear from his perspective I deserved nothing more than one curt look. My immediate reaction was "how rude," until

I remembered I was wearing a tacky Doris outfit. I snatched off the hat and fluffed my hair.

He was still unimpressed. "We deal only in gold, silver, and platinum. One deck down you'll find the tourist fare, much more suitable to your taste—and budget."

My mind raced for the exact words to defend my right to shop wherever I pleased. A subtly placed price tag on a ladies' gold watch inside the main display case caught my eye. $52,000.00! A cheap watch beside it: $8,975!

I plopped the turquoise hat back on my head, used one of the gold-plated mirrors provided for suitable customers to adjust my sequined, cats-eye sunglasses, and strolled out.

"Tourist fare," I mumbled. Still, it couldn't hurt to try.

I spun around and marched right back in. "Perhaps I should explain. My aunt, a stage and screen actress, Ethel Lipton, asked me to do some preliminary sleuthing. She is in need of a new watch. To her dismay, a jewel-encrusted watch, gifted by her dearly departed third husband, was stolen from her state room yesterday."

That got his attention. "Oh, dear. Has she notified ship security?"

"Oh, of course, they've been notified. As has her insurance carrier. However, she's lost without a watch and needs a replacement, ASAP."

"Hmph. I'm not surprised at this thievery. The riff-raff they let on board these days is disgusting." His demeanor changed from total disinterest to that of the cat preparing his attack on the canary. "How may I be of service? Do you think one of our high-end watches would soothe her despair?"

"Perhaps." I glanced at the watch display. "Would you happen to have something a little less ordinary? These are nice, but my aunt is used to *extraordinary*."

I imagined his pupils flashing dollar signs. "One moment. Let me show you what we have in the back."

I'd hooked him. Now all I had to do was successfully continue this little charade in order to pump him for information. He returned with a tray of gaudy watches. "I do so hope they catch those awful burglars, but in the meantime, would any of these be suitable for your aunt?"

I pretended to scrutinize each watch. "These are lovely, but she was so attached to the expensive one she had. I'm simply heartsick to think thieves are running rampant on such a quality cruise. Have you noticed anyone acting rather suspicious? Anything out of the ordinary?"

"Why, yes! I didn't witness the crime, personally, but there was a murder just the other night. In fact, I recognized the suspect from an article on the employee online newsletter. She had entered my shop. A rather crude and flighty woman. Her appearance was truly tasteless." He sniffed. "I instantly knew she was not a serious buyer."

No doubt he had described Ruby. "Did she say or do anything suspicious when she was here?"

He tapped his cheek with an index finger. "Hmm. No, but there did seem to be someone following her. The moment she left the shop, a woman, sitting on a bench outside, stood and followed her down the promenade."

A woman following Ruby? Ethel maybe, or one of the twins? Elbows resting on the counter, I leaned in. "Can you describe her?"

He shook his head. "I didn't see her face, but she was small, petite, with very dark hair."

Small? Petite? Nope, certainly not Ethel. Definitely not one of the twins. I leaned back and tapped the glass display case. "Well, I'd better be on my way."

Perplexed, the clerk huffed. "But…but what about your aunt's watch? You don't want to disappoint her, do you?"

I smiled. "Of course not. I'll bring her back so she can choose one of your lovely items. Good day."

Strutting out of the store, I imagined his face a flood of confusion. Continuing down the aisle toward the spa, I was convinced he had encountered Ruby, and perhaps a stalker. But why would someone need to follow her?

Three shops away, a ray from the late afternoon sun pierced the atrium ceiling pointing directly to a neon sign: *High Seas Beauty Salon and Spa*. "That's a little eerie."

I strolled to the reception desk where a plastic-looking honey-blonde with platinum highlights sat filing her nails.

She kept filing, barely disguising impatience for my unwelcome interruption. "If you want an appointment, we're booked solid through tomorrow."

Whoa, Miss Congeniality. She certainly found her calling. "I'm looking for a friend." I spotted a name plate on the counter. "Candee, is it?"

She glared, sighed, and stopped filing. "No, she's supposed to be here, but didn't show up, so I have to work a double shift. How am I supposed to find time to work on my tan if I'm stuck at this desk all day?"

I stopped short of reciting the dangers of sun exposure since any serious topic of conversation would be wasted on—

"And your name is?" I asked.

"Buffy Ann."

"Of course, it is." I put on my best smile that meant *you're a complete ditz, but I can't show it* and asked, "Did a passenger named Ethel make an appointment this afternoon?"

She stared vacantly at the appointment book. "Old, prune-faced lady?"

That would be Ethel. "Is she still here?"

"Guess so," Buffy Ann answered. "I think she came in for the works. Ha! There aren't enough 'works' in this place to fix her."

Although I'd pretty much thought the same—grouping myself in the judgmental category with that empty-headed bimbette—her insults were over the top. I swore to be more sympathetic and less critical in the future. After all, Ethel couldn't help the way she looked. Well, maybe if she stopped screwing her mouth up like she'd just sucked on a lime, but other than that, nature had not been kind.

"She happens to be my aunt." I lied, coldly, but without much effect on Buffy Ann's sensibilities.

"Whatever." She continued the serious task of manicuring.

"Excuse me." I tapped ragged edges of my chewed-up nails on the counter. "I need to talk to her. Can you tell me where she is?"

Buffy Ann pointed her file in the direction of a

curtained entrance on the left. "Through there, second door on the right."

"I can walk back there?"

"Suit yourself," she mumbled.

I slipped back through the vivid orange and chartreuse striped curtain and found a large bucket filled with cleaning supplies blocking the second door. "Hmph. So much for a fancy-schmancy spa."

I stepped back through the curtain into the lobby. "There's a Do Not Disturb sign on the door."

"I'm just here to answer the phone, lady. Check with the staff."

"And where might I find 'the staff'?"

She attempted a smile. "They're on a break."

"Why, thank you. You've been most helpful. I'll just bet, with your enthusiasm and ambition, you'll be running this place in no time."

She rolled her eyes and went back to, well, you know.

I shrugged. I could go into any one of those rooms, pretend to be a masseuse, and make some pretty good tips. Maybe another time.

Standing, again, in front of Ethel's door, I moved the bucket out of the way with my foot. Wonder if I should knock first? "Ethel? Are you in there?"

No answer, so I knocked, again, with no response.

"Ethel? It's me, Andi Anna. Ruby's stepdaughter. May I come in?"

Still, no answer. I turned the knob and pushed open the door.

A pungent chemical smell stung the inside of my nostrils. Squinting, I recognized the severe bun, black-dye job, and fleshy arms of the woman lying face-down on the massage table. Thankfully, a sheet tucked under her armpits covered most of her body. "Ethel? Are you awake?"

I stepped beside the table.

"Ethel?" Her head was lodged in the doughnut hole, so I put my hand on her cool shoulder and shook gently. No movement. Squatting on my knees, I peered under the table. The outline of a large nose pointed toward the floor. I fell backward from the fumes.

"Ethel! Wake up!"

Lightheaded, I got to my feet, grabbed her shoulders, and struggled to roll her onto her back. I instantly regretted my decision. Her eyes stared vacantly toward the ceiling. She was dead.

Chapter 12

I covered my mouth and nose with both hands and flew out the door to escape the noxious fumes. Dizzy, unable to think straight, I leaned against the wall outside Ethel's room. I couldn't just leave her there, but if I alerted security, they'd escort me off the ship for good. Not to mention joining Ruby as a prime suspect in another cruise ship death. My heart thumped and my breathing quickened to hyperventilation level. The first dead body I'd seen outside a funeral home, and it had to be someone I knew. I fumbled for my phone.

Thankful I had the forethought to put Manny's cell on speed dial.

"Sheriff Gonzales."

"Oh, thank God you answered," I whispered. "It's Andi, and I don't know what to do." My hand shook, making it difficult to keep the phone from clattering to the floor.

"What's wrong?"

I cupped my hand over my mouth and whispered, "Ethel's dead."

"What? Who?"

"Ethel Lipton, the witness you interviewed about Ruby and Lenny. I just found her dead on a massage table."

"Andi Anna, where are you?"

"I'm still on the ship in the High Seas Beauty

Salon & Spa on the main deck. I got a tip I had to check and, well, I met a dead end, pardon the pun. So, what do I do?" My instinct said to run.

"Stay there. I'm on my way."

"Stay here? With a corpse? Shouldn't you call 911?"

"Wait outside. I'll be there."

"But it will take forever for you to get here."

"Be sure you don't touch anything on the way out. Can you leave the spa without being noticed?"

I doubted Buffy Ann ever noticed much beyond herself. "Yeah, I'm sure that won't be a problem, but there's something else you should know."

"Tell me when I get there and stay close to the entrance without attracting attention. I'll be there as soon as possible."

I took a deep breath and slipped, once more, inside the room. The place was quiet as a tomb. Ironic, huh? I replaced the large towel over Ethel's body before leaving the room and shutting the door. Buffy was on the phone giggling with her back to me, and I tiptoed to the entrance.

I walked out as casually as my trembling body allowed and slipped into the adjacent shop—a bathing suit and lingerie boutique—to wait for the sheriff. How long would that be?

I wandered through rows of bathing suits, bras, and panties for fifteen or twenty minutes, making a conscious effort to slow my breathing and pretend to shop. I couldn't stay much longer without raising suspicion. Sure she'd spotted a potential shoplifter, the clerk's gaze followed my every move. I selected a lacy turquoise set and imagined wearing it on a real date with—

"I whole-heartedly approve."

Cramming the lingerie back in its place, I whirled around to face Manny. "I—how did you get here so fast?"

He moved around me and rested his arms on the rack. "I was already in Cozumel. I had this nagging feeling you'd need me before the day was over, so I hitched a ride with the coast guard." He gave me a curious once-over. "I barely recognized you in that, uh…outfit."

"What?" Uh-oh. The beach wear I borrowed from Doris. I sheepishly removed the hat and sequined sunglasses. "I was trying to blend in with the passengers."

"Good thinking." He lifted his arms off the rack, cleared his throat, and shifted to official business. "You might want to put them back on until you're in the clear with security. They know I'm here, supposedly to follow up on the previous murder. Once I've investigated, I'll tell Morrison we got an anonymous tip about a strange odor coming from the spa. Now, where's the most recent body?"

I motioned toward the spa. "Once you get inside, make a left and take the first door on the right. Should I stay here?" The way I figured, the lower my profile, the better, especially if Ms. Morrison got involved.

Before walking away, he asked, "Wasn't there something you started to tell me on the phone?"

What was it? Think, Andi. Oh, yeah. "When I got to Ethel's room, a cleaning bucket, filled with supplies, blocked the entrance. I opened the door, and a strong odor hit me, like maybe chlorine or ammonia."

"Interesting. Was the smell stronger near the body?"

I nodded. "The closer I got to her face, the stronger the odor. I almost passed out in there."

His eyes narrowed with concern. "Are you all right?" He grabbed his phone. "I'll call the onboard medical team. They can be here in less than a minute."

I pulled his phone down. "I'm fine. As soon as I left the room, my head cleared."

He smiled sheepishly. "Guess I overreacted."

I pictured throwing my arms around him, holding on forever. Instead, I quipped, "Maybe a little. Really, I'm good."

"Okay, I'll check the room out. Have you noticed anyone coming or going since you left? Or were you too busy looking inconspicuous?" He raised one eyebrow.

"I haven't seen anyone since I called you." I ignored the second question. "That place is like a morgue, literally."

I wanted to bite my tongue. I was so upset even dark humor couldn't lessen the tension. Manny either didn't hear my attempted joke, or he politely ignored me. Instead, he raised his cell phone for my benefit. "You stay here but call if you see anyone leave while I'm in there."

He slipped, discreetly, around the corner and entered the spa. I was sure Buffy Ann would be oblivious.

My cell rang. I answered, expecting to hear Manny's voice. "Wow, that was quick."

"Andi Anna? Oh, honey I'm free. I'm free!"

I gazed toward the ceiling. Perhaps guidance from

spirits experienced in handling exasperating stepmothers would swoop down and save my sanity.

"Who is this?" I asked. As much as I tried, I couldn't stop giving Ruby a hard time. Who am I kidding? I loved playing head games with her, even with the odds stacked heavily in my favor.

She chuckled. "Oh, you silly girl. I'm so happy to be out of that hellish place that I'm just going to let that slide. Not even your wisecracks can bother me, not today. I'm free!"

I pulled the cell away from my ear, anticipating the second shriek.

"Free, free, freeeeee!"

"I'm happy for you, but please don't scream again. Is Bert there with you?"

"Yes, he's right here."

A hushed and muffled conversation continued in the background.

"What's that, Bert?" Ruby came back on the phone. "He wants to talk to you, Andi, but first, did you get my clothes? Are you on your way here? Bert says he has to get back to the States and do some research on my case and, for some ridiculous reason, doesn't trust me on my own."

More muffled conversation in the background.

Ruby huffed. "Well, I never. Y'all are treating me like a child."

"Hey, sugar," Bert said, clearly having pried the phone away from Ruby. "What's the word? You on your way? 'Cuz I gotta run."

"Are the casinos calling you?" There was no way in hell Bert Bagley would leave without dropping at least ten grand at the gaming tables, or a weekend

Texas Hold-Em marathon I'd spotted in one of the tourist brochures.

"Heh-heh. Course not. I'm hurt you'd even suggest it. Like I told my little jewel here, I need to get her case moving and best if I begin the process in the States."

In the States? That made no sense. "Whatever you need to tell Ruby to keep her calm, handle it until I get back."

Ruby got back on the phone and rambled on about her clothes.

I wondered how Ruby would take Ethel's death. Should I tell Bert, or wait until I could be there to explain the details? Either way, hysterics were in the forecast. I walked to the front entrance of the boutique to get a good view of the spa. No sign of Manny. Part-time receptionist, full-time self-manicurist, Buffy Ann, busily screwed the top from what appeared to be bright pink nail polish. "It's a wonder her fingernails don't fall off in protest."

"What's that? Whose fingernails?"

I jumped, having forgotten I was still on the phone with Ruby. "Nothing, Ruby." My gaze shifted from side to side. No sign of security yet, but a young, male window washer appeared a little too interested in my conversation. The moment I looked his way, he lowered the bill on his ball cap and turned back to his work.

"Ruby," I said, "put Bert back on the phone."

I edged toward a bench in the center of the ship's atrium so I wouldn't be overheard.

"Bert, listen to me. I'm not sure you want to tell Ruby right this minute, but I think you should know that her friend, Ethel, is dead."

"What! Ethel Lipton's dead?"

A shriek rose in the background. "Oh, lordy! No, it can't be! My best friend? Oh, poor, sweet Ethel!"

Poor, sweet Ethel? After what Cloris and Doris told me, were Ruby's hysterics more show than sorrow? "Thanks a lot for your discretion. Is she okay?"

He tried to soothe the situation. "There, there, pumpkin, don't cry. Yes, sit down and drink this water. I gotta get back to Andi. Okay, she's calming down. Now, what the Sam Hill happened to Ethel? People are dropping like flies on that ship."

I couldn't argue. "The Cancun sheriff is here investigating right now. I'm waiting for him outside the spa where I—where Ethel's body was found."

Bert chuckled. "Oh, waiting for your lawman, hmm? The one that gets you all twitterpated?"

Ruby tee-hee'd in the background, so I assumed she was through grieving her dear friend.

"I'm simply waiting on the sheriff to complete his investigation. That's all. I called him because he's already aware of the relationship between Ruby and Ethel. End of story."

"Okay, okay. Didn't mean to get you riled up. Let me know what he finds out. You know, how Ethel died, and if it has anything to do with our case. All we need is another murder connected with this mess. Sorry, I mean this tragic death. Guess I'll wait here until you get back."

"You do that, Bert."

"Oh, before you hang up, I took the liberty of moving Ruby into your hotel room."

Swell.

Chapter 13

I slipped my cell back in my bag and turned toward the spa. Manny stood outside, frantically signaling. He mouthed, "Hide, hide!"

I slipped behind a large ficus, and a security team rushed toward him with Ms. Morrison in the lead. The conversation was barely audible, but the sheriff pointed toward the back where Ethel's body lie in undignified glory. Wonder if I should've left her face down instead of moving her on her back? *That was dumb, Andi!* I knew better than to tamper with evidence or move a body. I watched all those detective shows. Maybe I shouldn't have covered her torso with a bath sheet. Too late for second-guessing.

Buffy Ann reacted to the turmoil around her by blowing on the tips of her newly painted pink fingernails. Minutes later, as a medical team arrived with a stretcher, and I took the opportunity to hide behind a large potted bamboo plant closer to the entrance. Removing my neon-colored hat, I peeked between the leaves and shoots.

The hubbub finally brought the receptionist to life. Buffy Ann's eyes were the size of half-dollars. She was clearly irate at the interruption to her nail manicure.

Manny flashed his badge. I couldn't hear much more than a few words: police business, coroner. But "I need to speak to your manager" came through loud and clear.

Buffy Ann picked up the phone and punched in a number, probably her boss. Clearly nervous, her hands clenched the shaky receiver. "I don't know," she shouted for all to hear. "But the cops are here, and someone asked where the body was! No, I will not! I've already worked way beyond my shift. You need to get up here right now."

Who knew? Buffy had a backbone. Moments after she hung up, Ms. Morrison walked from the back of the spa followed by the sheriff, their heads bent together in serious conversation. The hairs on my neck prickled when two paramedics wheeled a stretcher and body bag from the spa. Another possible cruise ship murder victim? This one hit too close to home.

Poor Ethel. How did she get mixed up in Lenny's death? Or were they even connected? Before I let my imagination run wild, I needed Manny's opinion on the lethal nature of the chemicals. Could they have caused Ethel's death? Did she die from a heart attack? Considering the number one reason I came to Mexico in the first place—the murder of Lenny La Mour— natural cause was highly unlikely.

Security followed the stretcher onto an elevator. The sheriff waited until the doors closed before finding my hiding place behind the ficus. "Ms. Morrison will be occupied for a while, so I think you're in the clear. C'mon"—he grasped my elbow—"let's move away from the store fronts."

We hurried out to a mostly empty deck and sat facing each other on a couple of lounges. Electric currents shot through my body when our knees accidentally touched. *Not now, Andi! Ethel, remember?*

Dead body. Ruby, Lenny, rock-climbing wall, Bert, his white shoes, and nasty cigars. Okay, the last one did it.

"So, what's your conclusion? Was Ethel murdered, or do you think it was natural causes? She hasn't been in good health for years, according to Ruby."

"We should get a preliminary coroner's report within twenty-four hours. Not saying that will be the final report, but it should give us something to work with. The chemical smell in the room, though, was no coincidence. It appears she'd been dead at least three hours."

I told him about finding the brochure on the table. "Her appointment was at 1:30, so she'd definitely been there for some time."

"Doesn't mean she was dead all that time, but the coroner should be able to narrow it down." Heaving a sigh, he rubbed his eyes and put on his sunglasses. "What a day. Guess I'd better get back to the station. The coast guard won't wait around forever. Will you come with me? The boat glides through the water like a catamaran. We'll dock in Cancun in a half hour." He stood up, gazing down at me.

"Oh, yes. It'll save me from catching another taxi from Playa del Carmen. I needed a shower after riding in the back of the first cab."

"Great. I won't have to worry about your getting back safely." He smiled and took my hand, easily lifting me from the deck chair.

My relief I didn't have to make my way back to Cancun alone vanished when he asked, "Where are your stepmother's clothes?"

Rats! I'd completely forgotten about them. "Thanks for the reminder. I left the suitcase in the cabin across from Ruby's. I can't leave without it, or I'll never have any peace. Don't bother waiting. The twins may not be back, yet. As soon as I track them down, I'll grab Ruby's belongings and get to the ferry."

"Don't forget to return those stunning accessories before you leave." He cupped my elbow and sparks flew—again. "Wish I could wait, but I have to get back to file a report. I hate to leave you here. Are you sure you can make it to the ferry dock before 10:30? If not, I'm afraid you'll be here all night."

I checked my watch. "I should have plenty of time, as long as I avoid Ms. Morrison and her team." I said a reluctant goodbye, and he strolled out of sight. If only I'd remembered Ruby's stupid suitcase in the first place.

If I could envision the perfect scenario, Manny and I would speed across the bay, the occasional spray of water cooling our skin. His arm would be draped over my shoulder, pulling me close.

"Last call for the 8:00 p.m. dinner seating." The announcement not only pierced my eardrums, my romantic bubble burst like a glass balloon.

I trudged down the stairs to D-Deck and knocked on the cabin door. "Doris? Cloris? Are you in there?"

No answer. The girls must've left the afternoon tea buffet just in time for dinner. I thanked my lucky stars the cabin was unlocked and I wouldn't have to hunt them down. The thought of announcing Ethel's death made me ill. How did it happen? Four women leave on a cruise, excited and carefree. Three days later, one is in jail, accused of murder, and one is dead, face-down on a massage table.

No, I couldn't handle the anguish or the questions.

I'd also miss the last ferry to the mainland and have to bunk on the ship. I unzipped the jacket. "So long, beautiful purple cover-up. Adios, turquoise hat, the size of an extra-large golf umbrella. I'll miss you most of all."

After placing my borrowed beach wear neatly on the bed and the sunglasses on the nightstand, I grabbed the suitcase and plotted the fastest and least conspicuous way off the ship. The elevator. Ugh.

I was halfway up the hall when footsteps clomped down the stairway. The distinctive voice of Ms. Morrison rose above the low-pitched mumbling. "You couldn't watch one tourist? Do you have any idea if she's still on the ship?"

More mumbling.

"I don't want to hear excuses. Your one job was to make sure she was escorted off."

I ducked into an alcove containing an ice machine. Ms. Morrison and the humbled security guard flew past me. I waited for them to enter Ruby's cabin before I hurried to the elevator.

Whew! That was close. Relief when I cleared the elevator and the gangplank changed to anxiety realizing I was alone on the pier—a very dark pier. Bright lights from the ship did nothing to brighten my path. I glanced skyward. Rolling black clouds prevented any possibility of illumination from the full moon. Clutching my bag, I grabbed the handle of Ruby's suitcase with, thankfully, a superior rolling mechanism and sprinted toward the crosswalk leading to the ferry station.

I reached the main drag in record time and out of breath. A lone ferry waited to board a handful of tourists leaving the island after a full day of shopping and sightseeing. At least I wouldn't be crossing the bay alone.

I paid for a one-way ticket and dragged my exhausted body, along with Ruby's suitcase, up the ramp, vowing to get in better shape when I got home. No more sitting behind a computer all day and the TV all night. My condo was just blocks from the beach. I could walk five miles, seven days a week. Or two miles, three days a week. Or one mile, two days a week. *That sounds doable.*

The ferry was ninety percent empty. I considered sitting on the upper deck with most of the other passengers, but like my earlier trip, I settled safely below in a middle row. Waves lapped against the plastic-covered windows. My stomach churned. Too late for a seasick pill. If I took one now, I'd be close to the mainland before it kicked in. Besides, I'd had no hint of getting queasy the first time, so why bother. I shut my eyes and snuggled against Ruby's suitcase.

The engines revved, signaling our departure. "Ladies and gentlemen, our trip to Cancun could get a little bumpy. Please stay back from the rails. I'm sorry to add, due to the potential of rough seas, the bar area will be closed."

Rough seas? No seasick pills. No alcohol? I tilted Ruby's suitcase at a ninety-degree angle against the arm rest and stretched out on the hard, plastic bench. Ouch! Not good for a stiff neck. Not even close to nestling against the broad chest of a certain sheriff. *That ship has sailed, Andi.* Literally. I tried to relax, make the best of a bumpy trip.

We'd been at sea about fifteen minutes when the first wave hit. A wall of water slammed against the side of the ferry. The plastic curtains kept out most of the spray, but nausea hit me with the force of a killer whale's tail fin. Where were the restrooms? I'd spotted the sign after I boarded, but now dizziness challenged my sight, memory, and equilibrium. I tried to stand when another strong wave sent me tumbling across the deck.

Finding the restroom was no longer a priority. Finding a life jacket was. I'd heard an announcement about a storage locker near the front marked *flotation devices*, but when you're too sick to move, distinguishing bow from stern was the least of your problems.

"Señorita, can I help?"

Did I hear a voice? Mom? Dad? St. Peter?

Two hands reached under my shoulders and lifted me to a sitting position. I now knew the consequences of playing in a child's bouncy house. I swore when, or if, I got back to Florida, I would warn my sister to never let her kids play in one of those monstrosities.

"I have you," asserted a man's voice, "but we must get to the bow. Can you stand?"

"I—I think so." My knees wobbled, but with his help, I stayed vertical.

I stumbled along best I could, feet dragging, head spinning. I stayed upright thanks to the strong arms of a kind stranger. When we made it to shore, I'd be sure to thank him profusely.

He stopped and opened a door. "Here we are," he said. "You should have minded your own business, señorita. *Adios*."

Pushed roughly into a small space, I fell against the wall and sank to the concrete floor. The door slammed.

What the hell? My stomach churned. My neck flopped involuntarily. My eyes rolled like two ping pong balls on a tile floor.

A dim florescent light flickered on the ceiling allowing me to distinguish a door. Scraping noises and a loud thud coming from outside the room set alarm bells off in my brain. I struggled to stand, finally grabbing on to a porcelain sink and pulling myself upright. To the left was a bathroom stall. *Where was this when I needed it?*

I twisted the doorknob. It wasn't locked, but the door wouldn't budge. I banged with both palms. "Help! Help! Can anybody hear me?"

I reached for my cell phone to call Ellie—no, I should call Manny. But there was no cell phone. I forgot I stuck it into Ruby's luggage.

The ferry rocked violently and slammed me into the outside wall. Deafening waves crashed against the side of the boat. Water flowed underneath the door, first a trickle and then by the buckets. Something was scraping along the door and fell into it with a thud. "Hey! Is something blocking the door? I'm in here and the water is rising!"

I banged both fists against the door moments before another fierce jolt sent me tumbling backward under the sink. The spinning floor of a funhouse would've been less treacherous. Water churned around me, covering my feet and soaking my capris. Grabbing hold of the plumbing under the sink basin, I held on for dear life, shivering uncontrollably in surging water. My breathing got shallow. I searched for a porthole. The walls started closing. "Oh, no. Not now!" Even the chill of the water couldn't keep my neck and face from flushing signaling a full-blown claustrophobic attack.

I imagined the worst. The ferry would sink, or I'd drown before anyone found me. I could see the news headline: Tourist Drowns Under Bathroom Sink. I made an effort to stand, but the room spun. I fell back, pulled my knees to my chin, and wrapped my arms as tight as possible around my legs to stave off the cold moving up my body.

Do I really want to go this way? The preferred method would be sitting on the beach when I'm 108 years old, gazing at the ocean—a calm one, at that—drinking an iced coffee, most definitely with Manny. Now that was never going to happen. I was going to drown in the loo.

What was I thinking? I couldn't just give up. I crawled to the door, pulled myself up, and shoved my shoulder against the door as hard as possible. No luck. The ferry rocked sideways, sending me rolling across the room. My breathing was so shallow, I wasn't sure I could move. But that wasn't an option. I didn't want my epitaph to read, "Died in stinky boat head."

Ignoring exhaustion, I inched toward the door and shoved it with my last bit of strength Miraculously, the boat rocked forward at the same time. Whatever was blocking my exit shifted, allowing me to squeeze through the door.

Chapter 14

I was free! My eyes drew into focus, and the bile in my stomach calmed. Two heavy crates inched gently back and forth. The ferry had stopped its ferocious rocking. The worst was over.

My imprisonment in the bathroom was no accident I was sure of it. I had to get to the bow before my attacker came back. Prepared to crawl to the front, if need be, I managed to put one foot in front of the other and slowly make my way across the soggy deck.

Halfway there, a crew member approached. "Señorita, you need help?" I could only imagine the sight before him. A freshly bathed sheep dog? A large clump of seaweed…with eyes, nose, mouth perhaps? On the other hand, was he my previous assailant? His kind eyes and concerned look spoke differently.

He held my left hand and supported my waist with his right arm, guiding me to the front of the ferry. I marveled at the destruction. The plastic window protectors were ripped to shreds, benches strewn about, piles of broken bottles and paper cups littered the deck.

For some awkward reason, I needed to speak. "That was some storm, huh?"

He gave a wry smile to my understatement of the year and steered me toward a semi-dry bench.

Soon, another crewman spotted us and brought a couple of dry towels. "I'm sure the suddenness of the storm caught you by surprise, señorita, but didn't you hear the captain's instructions to come to the front? The stern was taking on water faster than it could be pumped out. Why were you in the back?" He rattled on about how plexiglass windows protected the bow while passengers held on to inside rails.

Sure, that made sense except I was trapped in the freaking bathroom because someone shoved me in there. But who? I recited the order of events, as much for my benefit as theirs. "As soon as the storm hit, I got violently ill. A man suggested helping me to the bow with the other passengers."

"Maybe he got turned around," said one of my rescuers.

"Then why would he shove me in the bathroom and block the door so I couldn't get out?"

I wasn't sure how much I should I reveal? Was it a good time to accuse someone of trying to hurt me—or worse? A report would be sent to the authorities concerning the storm and damage to the ferry, but what about the damage to me? Eager to get back to the safety of dry land, I heaved a relieved sigh when the docking process began.

"Do you think you can walk to the bow? We'll order a wheelchair when we dock."

Amazed by how quickly the nausea lifted once the reason diminished, I waved them off. "No, I'm fine, now. I can walk and have no need for a wheelchair."

I made my way to the front, unassisted.

"Señorita!" One of my rescuers ran to me carrying Ruby's ladybug suitcase. "Is this yours? We found it wedged under one of the seats and no one has claimed it."

"Yes, it's mine. Thanks, so much, for finding it."
Good grief, Andi. I could only imagine Ruby's fury if I
showed up without her precious items.

I exited the boat, dragging Ruby's suitcase behind.
But I paused halfway down, glanced slowly to the right
and then left. I had the uneasy feeling that someone was
watching my every move.

Sure enough, a thin man in a Miami baseball cap
turned away the moment we made eye contact. He and
the hat looked familiar. Before I could get a closer look,
he turned and strode toward town. Probably nothing,
but my guard was up. Anyone who looked my way was
now on my radar.

"You need ride, señorita?" The driver of the non-
descript vehicle I'd spotted earlier stepped forward, an
eager look in his eyes. "I drive you to town?"

The closer I got, the younger he looked. "Are you
old enough to drive?"

He smiled. "Oh, si, si. I drive for years!"

I glanced up and down the vacant pier. "Whip out
that license, kid, or move along."

He opened the driver door, reached across the seat,
and pulled a ratty wallet from the glove box. Holding
the license proudly between his thumb and forefinger,
he grinned. "See, official from state of Quintana Roo.
Good for five years."

Yeah, like he couldn't get a fake. I was, however,
desperate to get back to the safety of my hotel. I
squinted at the name printed on the card. "Okay,
Tomás, I need to get to Cancun as fast as possible."
Reconsidering my instructions I added, "Fast, but safe,
comprende?"

He nodded, took my hand, and helped me into the

back. Placing Ruby's suitcase on the seat beside me he said, "Sorry. Trunk no work."

Contrary to my earlier stinky ride, however, a clean and refreshing scent filled the car. I took out my cell to call Manny. No signal. I'd try again closer to Cancun. I wondered how he'll react to the attack. I backhanded Ruby's ladybug suitcase. "It's your fault. I could've taken the Coast Guard boat and avoided all this."

"What's that, miss?"

'Oh, nothing." I mentally recalled the story again so I could report everything that happened. This was no accident, and someone needed to take responsibility.

Another image, the stranger at the pier, eyes staring from under the ball cap, nagged at me. I'd definitely seen him before at a different time and place, even wearing the same hat.

Tomás broke my concentration. "Almost to Cancun, señorita. Where you want to go?"

I gave him the address of the hotel and dug out my key card. We pulled up at the hotel at 11:30 p.m. Tomorrow morning, first thing, I'd call Manny and relay the details about my harrowing trip. Tonight, my only priority was to collapse on a soft, tranquil mattress.

I dragged my aching body, along with the increasingly heavy suitcase, to my room and opened the door.

So much for tranquility.

"Andi Anna! It's about time you got here! What took you so long? I'm going out of my mind in these dirty old clothes!"

After what I'd been through, I summoned every ounce of energy to smile and be polite.

Bert, passed out in the easy chair, opened one bleary eye. "Wow! You look like the devil. Did you swim back from Cozumel?"

That did it. "No, I didn't, Bert. But how would you like to take a long leap off a short pier?"

"Whoa, sugar. I'm just stating facts. Looks like someone's in a pissy mood. Maybe I should leave you two gals alone to sort it out."

To my surprise, Ruby nodded. "That might be best. Give us girls a chance to catch up, and for Andi to get some rest. Lord knows she needs her beauty sleep."

Bert snorted.

I walked to the door and opened it wide. "Bert, you do whatever it is half-baked lawyers do in their spare time. Go back to your room, to the casinos, book passage on a slow boat to China. I really don't care. Just get out!"

He feigned hurt feelings. "Don't forget I flew all the way down here at your request."

"And right now, I'm regretting that decision. Out!"

He stood, grabbed his coat, and gave Ruby a peck on the cheek. "See you t'morrow, sweetheart."

A slightly subdued Ruby started to respond, but I gave her a sour expression and she slipped into the bathroom. Bert, wisely and quietly, exited the room.

I fluffed a couple of pillows, turned onto my side, facing the wall, and shut my eyes. Exhaustion did nothing to quiet my thoughts. Probably good I got home too late to call Manny. I mulled over how much to say in the morning without sounding hysterical. While my relationship with the sheriff was too new to rate, his professional competence was not in question. I knew he'd help sort out the details and get to the bottom of what exactly happened on the ferry.

On second thought, I'd sensed a lack of support for my trip to Vegas. *Should I listen to him? Find another way to get information?* Half of me wanted to pull the covers over my head and block out the world. But my stubborn, dominant half wouldn't cooperate.

Chapter 15

I must've fallen asleep at some point because the shower woke me around 9:00 a.m. Let me rephrase that. Wails from a tuneless rendition of "Memories" from the Broadway play, *Cats*, woke me. Ruby sounded more like a real cat losing all nine lives at once. "Ah-ha! The true meaning of caterwauling." I snorted, pleased my sense of humor was on its way back.

My positive mood was tested with the first stretch. Every muscle in my body ached. A deep purple bruise spread from my knee to my upper thigh. A tender right hip brought reminders of banging against the restroom wall. What I wouldn't give for a hot tub full of bath salts. Problem one: Ruby continued to occupy the shower. Problem two: I had no bath salts. I'd have to settle for a hot shower, if and when it was free.

I checked my phone for messages from Ellie. Nothing on my reservations to Vegas. I'd wait until I dressed to give her a call. Meanwhile, I packed my satchel for the trip to Las Vegas: clean undergarments, one light change of clothes, toothbrush, toothpaste, and makeup bag. Everything I'd need for a very quick trip to Nevada. *Oh, no!* It all came rushing back. I'd thrown Bert out last night and even suggested he leave the country. If he truly took my advice, who would stay with Ruby? I grabbed my cell and punched in his number.

"Yeah."

"Bert? Man, you sound awful. Please tell me you had a late night at one of the Cancun casinos."

"You got me. After you so rudely tossed me out, I popped into one Cancun casino. Actually, three of them. Happy?"

"Ecstatic! Don't go anywhere until you've heard from me. Understand?"

"But I'm hearing you right now. This doesn't count?"

"No, I'll call you later, after you've sobered up. And stay put." Whew, one problem solved. Relief he hadn't taken last night's angry words to heart mixed with disappointment he wasn't thousands of miles away. *Now to get Wendy Warbler out of the bathroom so I could get in.* Knowing Ruby's timetable revolved around her own convenience, I settled back in the chair to wait.

I thought back to the first time I'd met Ruby at Dad's request. He'd asked my sister, Georgia, and me to have dinner with him and his new girlfriend at a local Mexican restaurant. My sister was pleasant and courteous. Me? I dumped a margarita in Ruby's purse. What a waste! Wish I had one now. In fact, I wish I had the whole pitcher. Something, anything to deaden the sounds coming from the bathroom.

Finally, after a forty-five-minute concert ranging from the soundtrack of *The Music Man* to *South Pacific*, the shower shut off.

I knocked on the door. "Hey, Ruby, I need to get in there."

"But I haven't put on my face yet."

Oh, for the love of...

"I believe the light would be much better out here for applying your makeup. The harsh lighting in the bathroom makes you look ten years older."

The door flew open. "You really think so? Oh my, I can't have that." Grabbing her robe and three bags of paraphernalia, she sped from the bathroom. I sped in and locked the door. Never had warm, pulsating water felt so good. The bruise above my knee stung with contact, as did the welt on my right hip, but my sore muscles loosened with each wave of heat.

I wondered if I should I postpone my trip to Las Vegas? I dreaded sitting crammed in a plane seat, but if I didn't check out the main witness's newly discovered connection to Vegas, who would? I'd be shocked if the Cancun police department had the manpower or funds to designate a detective to check out a questionable lead. I certainly didn't have the money to hire a private investigator.

I shut off the water and stepped from the tub. Wrapping up in a fluffy white bath towel. A text had come in from Ellie saying the earliest she could get a flight to Vegas was tomorrow at noon. Some kind of problem with the incoming plane. I texted back.

—*Mechanical?*—

—*No. Scheduling*—

Okay, I could live with that. Mechanical problems and I don't mix. I'd rather saunter my way through the southwest on a pack mule than trust a broken-down aircraft. Great attitude from a travel agent, huh?

I'd gone from rushing to make my flight to having plenty of time to gather my thoughts between now and tomorrow. I debated whether to call Manny about my change of plans. Maybe he'd take the hint and suggest we meet tonight. On the other hand, what if he brushes me off? With such short notice, he probably had plans with another señorita. *Who am I kidding?* I'll bet the women were lined up, begging to be incarcerated by the handsome sheriff.

Maybe I'd sit by the hotel pool and relax for a while. Damn! That nagging sense of duty raised its ugly head. I'd have to take Ruby with me. As long as we stayed on hotel grounds, I saw no problem. On the other hand, the words *relax* and *Ruby* didn't mix. Maybe a tiny white lie was in order. I phoned Bert. "Hey, wanted to let you know I'm off to Las Vegas to check out a lead. You'll need to stay with Ruby."

"What? But I'm sitting here in the casino with an ace and feeling certain this pretty little dealer is fixing to send a big ol' face card my way."

"Oh, sorry, didn't realize. Of course, gambling takes precedence." My voice dripped with sarcasm.

"Oh, that's okay, sugar. Listen, I'll call ya back in a couple of hours."

That did it. "It's noon! Your Blackjack game can wait. Get over here—now!"

"But—but, oh hell. The dealer just got Blackjack anyway. No winners. Yeah, I'll be there in a few."

"A few minutes, Bert. Not a few hours."

"Hmph. Hope you're in a better mood when I get there."

Click.

So, I failed to tell him I wasn't leaving until tomorrow evening or that lounging by the hotel pool— without Ruby—was in my imminent future. *What he doesn't know won't hurt him.*

Better tell Ruby to listen for Bert. Wrapped up in

the other terry robe, I opened the bathroom door and a whoosh of steam poured out.

"My goodness gracious sakes alive," Ruby sputtered. "I just got my hair fixed. The humidity pouring into this room is going to ruin it!"

I bit my tongue to keep from reminding her nothing could deflate the bird nest piled on top of her head. "You and your hair will survive. Oh, and Bert's coming over—soon. Better finish getting dressed."

Digging a pair of white cotton shorts and white T-Shirt from my bag, I regretted not throwing in a bathing suit before I left Florida. Knowing Ruby and her ability to turn the simplest task, or carefree vacation, into a melodrama, I should've guessed the situation wouldn't be resolved in a day or two.

I jumped at the knock on the door. "Hey, open up."

Bert. I swayed between wishing he'd go away to relief I'd be free of Ruby for a few hours.

She rushed to the door. "Come in, you handsome devil, you." Batting her eyelashes, she planted a bright red smooch on his cheek. "I'm so glad you're here. I'm bored out of my mind. No offense, Andi."

"None taken," I assured her.

She played with the collar of Bert's palm print resort shirt. "Where are we going today? Maybe to one of those casinos? This twenty-dollar bill is burning a hole in my pocket. I just know my luck is going to change once I'm settled in front of a slot machine."

Would I have to tell her? No, Bert intervened. "Sit down, Ruby. Don't you remember you have to stay on hotel grounds? That's—" He pointed to her soggy ankle bracelet. "—the only way you could get bail." Taking a closer look, he added, "Good thing it's waterproof."

She folded her arms and made the face of a petulant six-year-old. "Oh, I might as well still be in jail."

That can be arranged. I stopped short of voicing my wish. No need to pile it on at this point. She'd be Bert's problem for a while. I gathered my phone, bag, and a bottle of water and headed to the door. "Oh, by-the-way, Bert, I'm not leaving for Vegas until tomorrow evening, but I have a couple of leads to check out before I go. See you later." A little white lie. But surely he couldn't blame me for wanting to catch some sun by the pool without Ruby prattling in my ear.

Whether the look on his face was surprise or annoyance, I'd worry about him after I'd recharged my batteries. Except for a window washer, bucket and squeegee in hand, the hall was empty. I turned my back and punched Manny's cell phone number on speed dial. No answer. I left a message and then called his office. He wasn't in, so I left my number. "Please ask him to call as soon as possible. No, it's not life or death, but I need to report an incident. No, I'd rather not talk to anyone else. Yes, thank you."

Whew, that was a bit awkward. I just hoped he'd call and soon.

Turning around to head for the elevator, the hall was empty. No window washer, no bucket, nothing. He must've moved to another floor.

Chapter 16

On the way to the pool, I stopped at the hotel's reservation desk and grabbed several brochures with enticing pictures of white sand, turquoise water, and, what else? Delicious restaurant meal choices. Oh, who was I kidding? I was in paradise and couldn't enjoy it. Not until I got Ruby out of this mess. But there was nothing more to do until I got to Las Vegas. So the pool it was but without dear old Ruby.

The pool area was crowded, but I spotted an empty lounge next to a water slide. I spread out one of the complimentary beach towels and plopped down. Compared to the bevy of skimpy bikinis and multicolored one-piece suits parading by, I had the style of a beached whale in my baggy shorts and T-Shirt. Had I interrupted a swimsuit photo shoot for a fashion magazine?

Speaking of scantily clad women, maybe Carmelita Vasquez was a model or showgirl in her day. Finding a list of performers and business associates of Lenny was imperative.

A water flume built around a fake rock waterfall created another distraction. Children and a few adults zipped around curves of rushing water. I considered taking a turn but would probably lose my shorts halfway down. *Where could I buy a cheap suit?* Certainly not in one of the cruise ship or hotel tourists' shops.

My cell buzzed. It was Manny. "Hola, Sheriff."

"Buenos dias, Andi. Your message sounded urgent. Is something wrong?"

How do I begin? "At the moment, no, but I need to talk to you about last night, and I'd rather do it in person."

"I can meet you later this afternoon. Say around 3:30 p.m. Will that work?"

I checked my watch. Noon. "Sure. Where do you want to meet?" I hoped he wouldn't suggest that cantina, again—or did I? Nope. Margaritas were off my radar for a while, maybe forever.

"We can meet at your hotel. How about the lounge?"

"I'll be there." *Drinking bottled water.*

I grabbed my towel and walked back to the hotel lobby. "Is there a concierge on duty?"

A young woman with the longest, fakest eyelashes I'd ever seen looked up from her computer. She could give Ruby a run for her money. More startling was the color of her hair, a shade of orange I'd never seen on the head of a human being.

"No, señorita, I'm afraid she's out at the moment. If you wish to book an excursion, you may leave a message. Someone will get back to you as soon as possible." She handed over several brightly colored brochures of private beaches, a Mayan temple, waterfalls, and even one for a flea market tour.

I listened patiently to her spiel. "Please tell her Miss Jones in room 432 would like some information on bathing suit shops in the area."

"Excuse me, señorita, did you say, Miss Jones?"

I nodded. "Andi Jones."

She reached under the counter and handed me a slip of paper. "This note was on my desk when I returned from my break. It's for you, Miss Jones."

I unfolded the paper and read the scrawled message: *Meet north of bridge in Old Cancun. News about ship murders. 1:00 p.m.*

"You didn't see who delivered this?"

A bit defensive, she replied, "No. I'm not required to be at my desk every minute."

"No offense. I was just asking." Great. I'd pissed off one of two people connected with this note. The other being the person who left it. I turned away and read it again. This couldn't be from Manny. We had just talked. *I'll check in with him, anyway.* Someone else needed to know about the note and where I was going. I hesitated. He'd probably try to talk me out of going alone. Maybe he could go with me. Have my back, just in case. I punched his cell number on speed dial. It rolled to voice mail. I called his work number. The same woman I'd spoken to before answered.

"Hola. This is Andi Jones calling for the sheriff again."

"Sheriff Gonzales is not available at the moment, Señorita Jones. Would you like to leave another message?"

"But I literally just got off the phone with him."

"Sorry, Señorita Jones. He left half an hour ago."

Should I risk going alone? The night before, I'd barely escaped with my life. The front desk clerk interrupted my thoughts. "May I get you a bottle of water?"

Guess she was trying to make amends for her early

curt response. "No, no, I'm fine. But I do need some information, please. Could you give me directions to Old Cancun?"

"I could, but I doubt I'd ever see you again. Trust me. Tourists should not wander outside the hotel and beach areas."

"Even during the day?" If I could navigate the streets and shops in Miami, the little old town of Cancun should be no problem. Besides, from all I'd read on the small city, the only way to experience true Yucatan culture was to venture away from the hotel district. She's probably trained to encourage tourists to only spend money at the resorts.

"Even in bright daylight, señorita. Please heed my warning. Stay away."

Clearly, she'd be no help. I wonder if my GPS could find the location? Good thing my hotel wasn't on the main tourist drag. I was on the far-left side of the number seven graphic that showed the long strip of commercial hotel properties. I moved to a wrought iron bench, across from the hotel clerk, and started a search. Sure enough, a map appeared showing the route to the old city. Not only that, a dozen or more shopping and restaurant options appeared. Most were in hotels, but Bren's Beach Boutique, several blocks away, caught my eye. "Bren's?" The name alone was worth checking out.

Maybe I'll combine business with pleasure. I walked back to the desk. "Is Bren's Beach Boutique close to the bridge in Old Cancun?"

She nodded. "Yes, it's a nice shop with reasonably priced items. Still, it's outside the tourist district."

I rolled my eyes.

"I can see you are not convinced, so travel at your own risk, señorita." The front desk clerk with her flaming orange hair turned and walked to the back.

I placed the straps of my bag across my chest. Clutching it—tightly—I strolled cautiously but confidently from the hotel following the instructions on the map. Getting out among real people—other than self-absorbed vacationers—lifted my spirits. My sore knee loosened up with every stride. The stores off the beaten path were neat and clean. Yucatan natives, families, couples, and singles moved in and out of the various shops from bakeries to footwear to restaurants. Street vendors called out in broken English. "Miss! You buy necklace. I sell cheap. Jewels from tomb of Mayan queen!"

Yeah, sure they are. I put up my hand as he raced toward me. "Sorry." I shrugged. "My great-great grandmother was Cleopatra. I got a lot of cool stuff from her."

I moved along to a small clothing store and peered through the window. Displayed were racks of jeans, denim shirts, plain blouses, and leather handbags. A few bikinis hung on the wall, but nothing I'd be seen dead in, or alive for that matter.

I continued down the street toward the bridge until the scent of pastries threatened to stop me in my tracks. I drooled at the window. Churros, flan, sopopillas, wedding cookies, all looked and smelled too good to pass up. Maybe on the way back I'd grab an empanada, a couple of desserts, and take them back to the hotel. What was I thinking? Shopping would have to wait. The mystery person could have clues that would free Ruby. Business first.

I checked my phone again. Almost 1:00 p.m. Nothing from Manny. The bridge was straight ahead. *Maybe he's waiting for me.*

I scanned the sparse crowd. What if he, or she, didn't wait on me? I did a 360 search of the area. Several street vendors closed in. I must have the word *tourist* stamped on my forehead. Looking back, I spotted Bren's Boutique on the left. Crossing the street, the colorful window display caught my eye. Fashionable swimsuits, elegant cover ups, and sensible beach hats. Good place to get away from sidewalk peddlers hawking everything from live chickens to brightly colored beach bags. I'd also have a good view of the bridge from the window of the boutique.

A lovely young woman greeted me when I ducked inside. "Hola, señorita."

Shocked by her appearance, all I managed to say back was "Hola."

Her flaming red hair stood out like a mirage in the middle of the Sahara Desert. Had I stepped through a portal and landed in Great Britain?

She chuckled. "No, I'm not from Cancun. Hi, my name is Brendolyn Shannon. You're American, right?"

I stuck out my hand. "Pleasure meeting you, Brendolyn, or should I say, Bren?"

"Either one. I've been Bren or Brennie since childhood. And you are?"

"Oh, sorry. I'm Andi Jones."

"So, Andi, are you here on business, or are you drawn to authentic Mexican food and wares?"

While scanning the bridge for signs of my informant, I pretended to be in Cancun on vacation and that I'd forgotten my bathing suit and wanted to find one that didn't cost an arm and a leg. "I'm curious about why you opened a shop in Cancun. How did you get here?"

She chuckled. "Long story short, I needed a change. After visiting several times, I fell in love with the culture and the people. You'd think, opening a new business, I would encounter resentment, but the merchants and residents welcomed me with open arms. That's why I'm here to stay. So, let's look for a bathing suit."

"That's what I'm here for." I made no mention of the note and continued searching the streets and bridge for the mystery person who lured me to the old part of town. Doubt crept into my decision to walk there alone. I checked my phone, again. No calls or texts from Manny. *What was I thinking?*

Deciding to walk back to the hotel and wait for our scheduled meeting, I turned around to tell Bren I was leaving but she'd moved to a rack in the back of the shop. "We have these one-piece suits," she said, "or several two-piece styles. But if you're looking for string bikinis, I'm afraid we don't stock those."

I hesitated. I should leave, but what would it hurt to look around for a minute or two? I really did need a suit. "Those look perfect." I joined her at the suit rack and flipped through several gorgeous colors and patterns, finally settling on a navy one-piece with lavender and lime stripes—vertical, of course, to slim the figure. Pleased by the price and slimming element, I asked, "Do you have this in a size ten?"

She thought for a minute. "Let me check in the back."

Happy for the chance to browse, I searched the

racks for capris and shorts. So many to choose! I gathered as many as my arms could carry and located two small dressing rooms in the back. Dismissing my original purpose for being there, and nagging fears I could've walked into a trap, I yelled to the owner, "I'm trying on a few things. If you find the suit in my size, hand it to me, please."

I listened for a response. None came. *Hmm, she must be rooting through boxes.* I entered the tiny dressing room through a flaming orange curtain and hung my items on hooks to the left. To the right was a mirror, barely wide enough to display both my hips at the same time. "The women down here must be skinny."

I selected a pair of sea-blue capris, a color and style suitable for both Miami seasons: hot and blazing hot. They fit like a glove. I chose a white gauze top and, *voila*, the perfect combination for work or play. While admiring the way the stretchy material smoothed my tummy, without creating the dreaded muffin top, the curtain fluttered. Busily deciding what to try on next, I stuck out my hand. "Did you find the suit? You have a great selection of—"

A vicious shove pinned me against the wall. The attacker's alcohol- and tobacco-tainted breath overpowered the tiny space. "Do not scream or fight, señorita, and you won't be hurt.

I nodded, afraid to speak, even if I could.

"*Esa es buena.* Now, listen carefully. Forget about the cruise ship murders, or you will suffer the same fate as the woman in the spa. *Comprende?*"

With my face still pressed against the wall, I was acutely aware of the tiny dressing room, and with the mention of Ethel, a mixture of panic and anger churned in my stomach. This man, whoever he was, had just threatened my life too. He either killed Ethel and perhaps Lenny or knew who did. But I had no choice but to cooperate. "Yes, I understand."

He shoved me again—for emphasis, I supposed. "You are very smart, Miss Jones. Forget this ever happened." He slipped through the curtain and was gone.

My legs gave out. I slumped to the floor. Hearing nothing inside the shop but my heavy breathing, I peeked from behind the curtain. Fear for my own life subsided, concern for the shop owner intensified. How did the intruder get past her? Surely she wasn't still in the back, unaware of what just took place. I scanned the area and tiptoed on wobbly legs to the back of the store.

Bren had her back to me, humming and going through inventory. My fear diminished—slightly—at the sight of her. She was blissfully unaware a dangerous man had entered the store and attacked a customer. She turned to grab a stack of casual shirts and jumped. "Oh, my! I didn't hear you. I see you found a nice outfit. Looks great on you."

I took a minute to process her words. Oh, yeah, the capris and top I was admiring in the mirror seconds before I was slammed into it.

"I…uh."

I took a breath and collected my thoughts. Should I tell her what happened? Should we call the police? And tell them what? A man snuck into the dressing room and threatened me? "No, sorry officer. I didn't see him. How tall was he? Uh, I'm not sure. Clothing? Nope. Didn't see what he was wearing, but he did have very bad breath." I doubt they'd be impressed with my description. And, since Bren wasn't involved, I decided to keep it that way.

"Yes, I'd like to check out."

She smiled. "Are you planning to wear that, or would you like to change and meet me up front?"

"I'll change." I tried to laugh, but a sick croak was all I managed. A couple of deeper breaths helped my body relaxed. My legs regained strength, and I'd stopped shaking. "I'll just be a second."

Before going back into the dressing room, I checked the store to be sure I'd have no more surprises. The small shop was empty. I peeked through the curtain. No one hiding in there either. Somehow, I got dressed and took my purchase to the front to check out.

"Just these two, huh? Didn't you come in looking for a bathing suit?"

"No, sorry. This is it." I had no desire to linger. Swimwear would have to wait.

I took my package and walked to the door. "Take care, Bren."

"You, too, Andi. Come back anytime."

Chapter 17

I hurried back to the hotel, my gaze scanning the sidewalks for anyone the least bit suspicious. I wished I'd gotten a good look at the scumbag. "Well, Andi, you wanted an excuse to talk to Manny. Now you have two." Not exactly a romantic interlude, but he needed to know what happened, not only today, but last night on the ferry. I'd be hard-pressed to believe both incidents weren't connected to the murder investigations. As much as I wanted to see him, I dreaded the lecture I'd get for striking out on my own.

Once safely in my room, I breathed a sigh of relief that Bert and Ruby were elsewhere. Whether still on hotel grounds, or not, was their problem. I'd been locked in a bathroom last night and threatened within an inch of my life today. I checked my watch. I had ten minutes before I met Manny. I quickly changed, grabbed a bottle of water, ran a brush through my hair, and tried to slow my pounding heart. At least I had an outfit.

I made it to the lounge a couple minutes early. I should harness that enthusiasm for days I had to drag myself to work. With no windows to provide natural light, I wasn't sure whether Manny was there or not. Given the sheriff's dazzling qualities, I was sure to spot him instantly once my eyes adjusted.

A shadow filled the doorway. No mistaking the

broad shoulders, trim waist, long legs, and muscular thighs. I think I actually gasped at the sight. He smiled and waved when spotting me sitting at a table in the back.

"Looks like you're hiding back here," he joked.

"If you only knew." His hazel eyes almost made me forget why I was there. "I need your professional feedback."

He pulled out a chair. "Uh-oh, sounds serious. Something to do with your stepmother?"

Ex-stepmother! Oh, why bother correcting him. No one appreciated the significance but me. Let it go. "I wasn't sure after last night's experience, but today's encounter was no coincidence."

"Last night? Did something happen on the ship after I left? When did you get back?"

"If you'll be patient, I'll start from the beginning." I filled in the details about having no problem finding Ruby's bag, slipping off the ship, unnoticed by security, and getting to the ferry dock. "Everything seemed normal. We were due to land in Playa del Carmen in just over a half an hour. That's when all hell broke loose."

I relayed as much as possible—the storm that hit the ferry, the man who offered to help me to the bow and ended up shoving me into the restroom—but without detailing my claustrophobia and bout of nausea. "I know he did it on purpose because his last words were 'I should've minded my own business.' Then I assume he blocked the door with a heavy storage cabinet to make it impossible to open."

"What? Why would someone do that? What did he look like?" The rise in his voice prompted strange looks from the bartender and handful of patrons.

"Uh, you might want to keep it down," I suggested.

He pounded the table. "I'm furious! I never should have left you last night."

"You're not to blame. No way could you predict the weather or that I'd be assaulted. Besides, there is much more to the story, and I need an objective opinion."

"I'm all yours." He crossed his arms on the table and leaned forward. "But first, were you hurt?"

After his earlier outburst, I decided to skip the details of my injuries and near drowning. He laid his hands over mine sending sparks shooting up my arms.

"Just a few bumps and bruises. Nothing to worry about. But as I was leaving the ferry, I spotted a man staring at me. The moment we made eye contact, he turned and hurried toward town. I never saw him again."

"Can you give a description?" Manny reached into his pocket and pulled out a small pad and pen. "We also have arrest photos you can look through."

I shook my head. "No, unfortunately, I don't remember much other than a black ball cap. I couldn't see the color of his hair, but he looked familiar. I'm not sure why. It's not like I'd ever seen him before, but something clicked."

"Was there a problem getting back to your hotel from the ferry dock?"

I assured him my ride back to Cancun with the young driver had been pleasant and uneventful. "Something, more sinister, however, happened today."

He sat back and took a deep breath. "Mind if I order a beer?" For clarification he added, "I'm off duty until tomorrow afternoon."

He flagged a server and asked for the house special on tap. I held up two fingers. Then he turned to me. "So, let's hear it."

I pulled out the message I'd gotten at the front desk. "I assume this didn't come from you because you had just called me."

He read the note. "Not from me and definitely not my handwriting. Could the clerk identify the person who left it?"

"That was my first question. She was on break and found it when she returned."

He leaned forward. "Well, at least you were smart enough to ignore it."

I bit my lip to fight the heat rising to my cheeks.

He fell back against the booth. "You didn't!"

"I thought I'd be safe. It was just a few blocks." I also failed to mention my stubborn defiance of the hotel clerk's warning. "The stores were neat, and the people were friendly looking. I had nothing to fear, or so I thought."

Those bedroom eyes narrowed. "Go on."

"Besides, I did leave you a message before I left."

"The message was that you'd called. No mention of where you were going. If I'd known, I would've stopped you or hunted you down." His jaw visibly clenched. I knew I was in trouble. "*Mujer loca*," he mumbled.

I ignored the apparent reference to my mental capacity and explained how I had ducked into Bren's Boutique in order to watch the bridge from a safe distance—and do a little shopping in the process. I motioned to my new outfit, hoping to break the tension, but his demeanor, seriously pissed, stayed unchanged.

"Anyway, the owner was in the back looking for a certain item, so I went into one of the dressing rooms to...try on this pair of capris and—" Well, no need to mention the arm-full of clothes I lugged in with me. "That's when I saw the curtain in the dressing room ruffle and thought it was the owner. Instead, a man charged in, pinned me against the wall, and—"

Manny almost jumped off his chair. "And what? Did he assault you?"

"He told me to stop digging into the cruise ship murders, or else I'd end up like Ethel. I didn't fight him, just went along with whatever he said. The moment he left, I went searching for the owner. She was unharmed in the back of the store, oblivious to what had just taken place."

Manny let loose with a string of Spanish I had no desire to translate. His hands gestured wildly. A couple at the bar stared with mild curiosity. Finally, after a five-minute tirade, he calmed down. "I don't usually lose my composure like that, but—my apologies, Andi."

Genuine fear was in his eyes.

"No need to apologize. I'm sorry for making such a bonehead decision to go off on my own and for putting my life and the shop owner's life in danger."

He squeezed a lime slice into his mug of beer and took a huge gulp. "I hate to ask, but did you call the police?"

I looked up sheepishly. "No. I didn't see the need since I couldn't identify him. As to the owner, she's fine. I didn't let on what had happened. No need to get her involved."

"So, you weren't able to get a description?"

I sat back, relieved he was no longer cursing in Spanish. "He had me plastered against the wall the whole time. Other than extremely bad breath…no."

Manny surprised me by taking both my hands in his. "I hate that you feared for your life. Now, let's get busy and try to find these assailants."

"Rest assured, I'm not leaving this hotel until they're caught. Hell, I may not even be safe here!" I shivered. The incident on the ferry was disturbing. The threat, delivered while being physically restrained by an unknown assailant, launched my fear to a new level.

"I assume this means you've given up the idea of flying to Las Vegas."

Uh-oh. Vegas. The plan to go it alone in a strange city was less appealing today.

"I—I was waiting on air and hotel suggestions from my assistant."

"So, you have no firm plans? Good. I plan to talk you out of going altogether. I wish we could spare one of our detectives, but there's simply not enough evidence to warrant the expense. Tell you what. I'll call my Vegas connection looking into Carmelita Vasquez and see if he can find something. Meanwhile, I will assign a guard outside your hotel room." He downed the last of his beer and snapped his fingers.

I felt better already, knowing Manny had my back in Cancun. How could I tell him I changed my mind and still wanted to fly to Las Vegas?

We walked back to my room. By the high-pitched laughter coming from within, I knew Ruby and Bert were back.

"One moment, please." Manny excused himself

and made a call. I waited outside the door, trying hard to keep Ruby's voice from grating on my nerves. "Okay, you're all set," he said. "A guard will be here in a few minutes. Do you want me to go in the room with you?"

I pictured Bert's raised eyebrows and smirk if I walked in with *my sheriff* in tow. "I don't want to excite Ruby. She'll think you're here to take her back to jail."

He chuckled. "After spending more than a day with your ex-stepmother, I have no doubt she'd overreact." He shuffled his feet and looked away. The awkward silence grew. Finally, he gave my shoulder a light squeeze. With the other hand, he raised my chin.

My eyes widened. I took a deep breath and prepared for the inevitable kiss on the lips.

Instead, he turned my head gently and brushed his lips against my cheek. "I'll hear from you tomorrow, right?"

"R-r-right." My face burned with a combination of desire and disappointment. Instead of bathing in the afterglow of a passionate kiss, I prepared to face my roomie and her lawyer.

Chapter 18

Ellie texted my flight and hotel reservations early the next morning. I had a few hours before I broke it to Bert that he'd be on Ruby guard duty for the next few days. Who was I kidding? Telling Bert was child's play compared to convincing Manny I could handle myself in Vegas.

Ruby was busy sipping coffee and watching her morning shows. I squinted out the security peep hole in the door and spotted a man in a blue uniform keeping watch and drinking from a large coffee to-go cup. Good thing he brought his own coffee. Ruby would pout if she had to share her morning brew. It was bad enough I snuck a half of a cup. The room service coffee was awful anyway. I usually waited until I could get a freshly ground latte. *Yes, I am a coffee snob.*

While Ruby was occupied, I took my shower. For some weird reason, I felt better calling Manny after I was clean, dressed, and with makeup applied—as if he could see through the phone. I poured another half of a cup while my roomie snorted over some game show contestant leaping around the stage during a jackpot-winning celebration.

I smiled and picked up my phone. I had stalled long enough. I had to talk to Manny. I slipped back into the bathroom for privacy—and to shut out the blaring TV. Maybe he'd be out. No such luck.

"Hola, Andi. *Como está usted?"*

"I'm fine, and you?"

"Better after hearing your voice and knowing you are safe in your room with a guard at your door. Yes, I checked early this morning, just to be sure he was on duty."

"I saw him too, although I don't think Ruby has. She'll probably be furious thinking he's here to keep her from leaving the hotel."

Manny chuckled. "Let her think whatever she likes. I'm relieved. So, what are your plans for today? No more exploratory adventures I hope."

I swallowed, hoping to clear the lump in my throat. "That's why—" I hesitated. "—I called. I just got confirmation for my trip to Vegas."

Silence.

"Are you there?"

He sighed. "Si, I'm here. Is there no way I can talk you out of going?"

"Probably not. Did you hear from your contact?"

"Not yet, but I didn't expect to so soon. These things take time, you know. Even when professionals are at work."

"I know, meaning I'm an amateur. I promise to keep you in the loop and take no unnecessary risks." He stayed silent, so I added, "I can't rest until I do everything possible to locate information on Carmelita Vasquez: where she's been and what she's up to. Ruby's life could depend on it."

"I do understand your passion and your stubborn need to strike out on your own. Please, just swear you'll be careful. Have you called anyone or made contacts?"

"The plane lands in Las Vegas at 2:50 p.m. local

time. I'll check in at the hotel—it's the one that looks like an Egyptian pyramid—and then contact a Lieutenant Glass. I hate to admit it, but I looked his name up on the internet. He popped up as lead detective in the Las Vegas entertainment area."

"Of course. When in doubt, google."

The sarcasm was not lost on me. I chose to take the high road. "If you think of someone who might help, let me know. I'm not afraid to admit I'll need it."

"I'll call my contact and give him your arrival time. Maybe he can meet you at the airport or hotel. Let me know when you arrive."

"Thanks, Manny, and don't worry. I'll be fine."

"Before you go, I was hoping—" He hesitated. "Adios, Andi."

"Wait! Manny, give me your contact's name." Too late. He hung up. Was he about to ask to see me before I left? Well, I couldn't let him distract me anyway. I had one more giant task ahead: getting Ruby situated. After a less-than-satisfying call to Manny, I was in no mood to spar with Bert.

"Hey, sugar. What's cooking?"

"I'm leaving for Las Vegas this afternoon and need you to look after Ruby."

"Overnight? That pull-out sofa aggravates my sciatica."

"Huh? You mean you and Ruby aren't—"

"Nah, we're just friends. Can't believe she didn't tell you. Not that I haven't thought about it from time to time, but she's a bit too fussy for me, if you know what I mean."

"I can imagine. Well, sorry about the accommodations, but it's the best I can do. So, I'll need to leave here in a couple of hours. Be here before then."

"But…I have errands to run, places to go, people to see."

Hmph, errands. *I'll bet.* "Just be here, Bert. If Ruby leaves, you'll be responsible for tracking her down."

That did it. He mumbled a few choice words before hanging up. I went back to packing.

Chapter 19

The jet took off, along with my blood pressure.
You'd think owning a travel business would help calm
my anxiety of flying in a small, enclosed metal tube. I
sat back and buckled my seat belt, hoping to relax, and
not let my claustrophobia take over. No such luck.

I focused on Yucatan landscape out the airplane
window, hoping to shed the suffocating waves crashing
over me, and tried to breathe through it. Other anxieties
piggybacked on my fear of confined places. What on
God's green earth made me think I could leave Ruby in
Bert's hands? I'd have to hit Vegas running to get the
scoop on this Carmelita person, so I could get back to
Mexico. When I did get back to Cancun, would Manny
ever speak to me again?

Sadness overwhelmed me as I left the beaches,
five-star hotels, casinos, margaritas, and especially the
Aztec godlike sheriff. Guess I should be grateful I
experienced my margarita hangover with Manny. After
his adios, I imagined I would never see him again.

The far-off blue of the Gulf out my window was
replaced by a set of hazel, bedroom eyes. *Oh...don't go
there, Andi.* The five-hour flight would be far more
productive reviewing notes.

Let's see. Priority one: get access to casino records.
Maybe they would uncover where the mystery witness
against Ruby had been hiding out for the past five

years. I hoped Lieutenant Glass would steer me to personnel records or to someone who had worked with Lenny. I wondered how I was supposed to get in touch with Manny's contact. I guessed he'd let me know after I got to Vegas if he was still speaking to me.

Whew. I was so tired. Still paying for that horrible ferry boat trip, I closed my eyes.

Umm...don't stop. Soft lips nibbled my neck as my dress slipped down over my hips and gathered at my feet. His cologne, an earthy mixture of spice and bay leaves, invaded my senses. His strong hands placed me delicately on silk sheets. "*Eres muy hermosa*, Andi."

"Ladies and gentlemen, to prepare for landing at McCarran International Airport, please make sure your seat belts are fastened."

I startled awake. My body was soaked in sweat.

"Miss? Miss, are you all right?"

My head spun toward a man across the aisle. "Oh, yes. I'm fine."

"I was a little concerned when you started moaning, and you look flushed. You don't have the flu, do you?"

I blushed and sat up. "No, really, I'm fine. Got all my shots. Nothing contagious. I just got too warm under, you know, the blanket," I mumbled, holding up the evidence.

Yeah, I got too warm, but not from the blanket. Anyway, my explanation seemed to satisfy him. I wiped sweat from my forehead and turned toward the window.

As the plane prepared to touch down in Las Vegas, I marveled at the miles and miles of casinos cluttering the city—including the massive pyramid, my destination. It was a city filled with so much excitement and entertainment. Pity I couldn't enjoy it any more than I did Cancun.

We landed smoothly and taxied to the gate. Grabbing my carry-on, I smiled at the man across the aisle, looking as healthy as possible to reassure him I was germ-free.

We must've landed during off-peak hours since I sped up the ramp, through customs, and out the airport doors. The suffocating Nevada heat caught me by surprise. Sure, I'd heard clients describe the weather, but they'd left out the "gasping for breath" consequence. Not only that, but I could feel my skin wrinkling in the low humidity. "Thank goodness for moisturizer."

Speaking of being dry, failure to stop for a cool drink before I left the airport was a big mistake. Even a germ-filled water fountain sounded good at that point. My scratchy throat would have to wait until I reached the hotel.

Hailing a cab was no issue. The moment I walked out of the airport, two pulled up simultaneously; one behind the other. A small man in the first cab rolled down the passenger window and asked where I wanted to go. Before I could answer, another driver in a Miami baseball cap jumped from the second car and brusquely signaled to the other driver. The first cabbie shrugged and moved on to another fare. "Where can I take you, Miss?"

I froze for a moment. Of course, he couldn't be the guy from the ferry. I was surely being paranoid. He said the name of the hotel and opened the back passenger door. "Any luggage?"

"No, just"—my voice came out in a croak—"this."

Before pulling out, he asked, "Are you all right, Miss? You sound like me when I had bronchitis a couple of months ago."

What is it with everyone thinking I'm sick? I managed to produce enough saliva to reply, "I'm fine."

He looked in his rearview mirror and nodded.

I settled back and marveled at the casino lights, shining bright in the middle of the day. "Oh, I envy you, Jonesy," Ellie had gushed when I'd called to let her know I was boarding the plane. "I've always wanted to go to Egypt." But I wasn't traveling to Egypt, I'd reminded her. Not to mention, I was on a pauper's budget, and our meager discounted rates weren't much help. "Oh, you know what I mean. It's the next best thing." I knew better than to argue with her. Besides, I'd requested the heart of the strip with access to all the major casinos, and she'd come through.

After a shorter-than-expected cab ride, we pulled up to the hotel. I had to admit, Ellie out-did herself. The hotel entrance was pretty darn impressive although the giant Sphinx kind of creeped me out.

"It's even prettier at night," the driver said, "when the blue lights shine from behind. If I were you, I'd be sure to check out the city after dark."

Considering the past few days, I wondered if he was coming on to me, or worse, planning an attack. *Stop being paranoid, Andi.* I paid the fare, including a modest tip, grabbed my carry-on and laptop, and slid from the back seat of the cab.

The driver stepped out and removed his cap revealing an impressive head of hair. "Enjoy your stay, Miss."

His translucent blue eyes stopped me cold. Instead of sexy bedroom blue, his cold glaring gaze suggested those of a hitman. "I…well, thanks for the suggestion about the lights, but this trip is more business than pleasure, I'm afraid."

"If you need a ride anywhere, ask for Diego. Here's my card." He walked around the taxi to the sidewalk and loomed over me. "Day or night."

I stuck the card in my jacket pocket. "Sure…Diego. You'll be my first call." *If Freddy Krueger's busy.*

Moving briskly toward the entrance to the hotel, I glanced over my shoulder to be sure the creepy cabbie didn't follow.

I entered through massive doors and into a gigantic pyramid filled with magnificent statues, a reflecting pool, and luxurious leather seating.

"King Tut couldn't have thought this up." Agency clients had tried to describe the opulence of the hotel and casino, but one had to see it to believe it. Middle Eastern fragrances drifted from a nearby restaurant: a mixture of fennel and coriander.

A couple dozen people were checking in as I approached one of the twenty, or more, stations behind the long, curved reception counter.

A young woman smiled on cue and welcomed me to the hotel and casino. "I'm Ashandri. May I have your name, please?"

"Andi Jones. My assistant made a reservation for me. I believe it's for two nights."

The young woman brushed midnight-black locks behind one ear and tapped information into her computer. "Ah, yes, Miss Jones. We have you booked into a one-bedroom tower suite. If you need more room, however, I'm sure we can change it to two-bedrooms."

A suite? What was Ellie thinking? "I just need a plain room. A bed, a phone, maybe a TV. I'll be out most of the time, so there's really no need for—"

"Miss Jones, it's complimentary. There's no extra charge to you."

"But I don't understand." A few of my clients had stayed in fabulous accommodations, but I didn't qualify for the high-roller category. "Is this a normal service?"

The young woman lowered her gaze and tapped the keyboard. "I have no more information for you other than you've been awarded a complimentary upgrade. I assume you won't need assistance with your luggage." She scrutinized the small travel bag slung over my shoulder and the laptop case in my right hand and handed over my room card with a flick of the wrist.

"I—"

"Have a wonderful stay, Miss Jones." Ashandri turned and strolled into a back room.

Okaaay. She'd be no help. Might as well see what this suite looked like. Before stepping into one of many elevators, I punched the agency speed dial. "Ellie. Give me a call ASAP."

I'd held my breath the entire trip during the enclosed ride to the twenty-eighth floor; fortunately, it only took mere seconds. Plush green carpeting and richly wallpapered halls led to my suite. While fumbling with the key card, my peripheral vision caught movement to my left. The moment I turned to look, a door clicked shut. A full-body shiver began at my heels and settled at my hairline. *Just your imagination, Andi.* Imagination, or not, I turned the deadbolt and flipped the safety latch for good measure.

The size and beauty of the suite took my breath away. Never could I dream up a plush violet-colored sofa and a TV as big as my car. There was a king-size bed and hot tub in a second room, along with another TV tucked behind the doors of a gigantic dresser and wardrobe. The pyramid-slanted windows offered a perfect view of a cloudless sky.

"Ellie, you done good." I placed my puny travel bag on the dresser and checked out the bathroom. "Holy cow! I could stay here for six months."

A mirrored wall accented a tub and gorgeous tiled shower with matching vanities. What a dream! Such a shame I couldn't share the opulent decor with someone special.

Arms spread, I fell back onto the bed, tucked a couple of squishy pillows under my head, and imagined I had nothing to do but live there, order room service, and watch TV while soaking in the hot tub. If only. First, I texted Ellie to let her know the room was great, and to thank her for taking care of my travel arrangements. Rather than describing the accommodations, long-distance, I'd take bunches of pictures to show her when I returned to Florida.

Much as I wanted to soak in the ambiance of my suite, I needed to hit the ground running. Planning what was left of my day was imperative.

I grabbed a notepad and pen from the desk. *Hmmm, should I sit there, or would I think better in the relaxing water of the hot tub?* The hot tub won, hands down. (You knew it would!)

I grabbed a sparkling water from the mini bar and climbed in wearing nothing but my natural birthday suit. Nothing between me and the outside world, except a huge piece of glass, would normally make me anxious. Thanks to the angled pyramid windows, however, the only Toms capable of peeping would require hot-air balloons, airplanes, or a super-duper telescope on the International Space Station.

The water temperature was a perfect one hundred degrees. Warm enough to soothe muscles but cool enough to keep my body from overheating. The day was going on 4:00 p.m. Mountain Time, and the sky took on a hazy hue. I dreaded going out but knew from word-of-mouth, I'd adjust to the desert heat.

A few minutes with the tub jets blowing full-speed on my mid-back and neck would do the trick. *Let's see.* My priorities: calling Detective Glass, locating a list of dancers employed by Lenny La Mour, and discovering Carmelita's whereabouts. Or was there something else I needed to do first. Manny's final words, "Let me know when you arrive," came through loud and clear. I dried off and snuggled into a luxurious cotton bathrobe.

I hesitated, my finger resting on the speed dial. I wondered if he'd acknowledge my call, or would he still be too upset by my trip to answer.

I worried for nothing. After one ring, "Hola, Andi."

"Hello, Manny." *Whew. No edge to his voice.* "Is this a good time to talk?

"Si. I was just about to take an afternoon break since I'm on duty until late this evening. What's up? Have you talked to the local police?"

"Not yet," I admitted. "I'm getting ready to call the local detective who specializes in missing persons' cases."

"Ah, yes. The one you *googled*."

146

Hmmm, maybe he is a bit edgy. "Don't you think Carmelita Vasquez would qualify since she disappeared off the face of the earth more than five years ago?"

"That's a good place to start." The tension in his voice eased, a bit. "I hope you don't mind, but—" He cleared his throat. "—my friend and contact in Vegas might stop by to see you."

"Have you told him about the case?"

"Si. He works undercover as a private investigator. Detective Ruiz. I gave him your itinerary and the specifics of your trip. If you need anything, please call him."

He gave me his friend's contact information and made me swear to call if I got into trouble. "Oh, I almost forgot. He said to eat at the…let's see. I have the name right here. Oh, yes. Eat at the Spicy Sphinx in the hotel. The restaurant employs several former showgirls. In fact, he said some have been there for a quarter century. You might get the inside scoop on Lenny or Carmelita."

"I can do that." Kill two birds with one stone, especially since I'm starved.

"And please, call my friend. Promise?"

"I promise. If Detective Ruiz doesn't call soon, I'll get in touch with him." After saying goodbye, I dressed for comfort. A pair of white cotton capris, purple tee with the sleeves rolled up, and white canvas slip-ons. Taking a bottle of water from the fridge, I left the luxurious suite to search for evidence on the elusive Carmelita Vasquez.

Chapter 20

Now, to find this wings place and get some food! And of course, start my search. While I didn't travel a thousand miles to eat, low blood sugar could stymie my ability to think on my feet.

I strolled through the hotel food court and passed Rose's Cantina, The Deli, Irish Pub—*Ah-ha! I found it!* The Spicy Sphinx. Before walking in, I placed a call to Lieutenant Glass.

"Sorry," answered a grumpy male voice. "He's gone for the day."

Click.

Okaaay. Guess I didn't want to leave a message. I hoped it wasn't an omen signifying the rest of my trip. I'd call after I ate on the chance of reaching someone with professional skills.

A server pointed me to a two-person table on the perimeter with a good view of the activity. You'd think five in the afternoon would be dead, but throngs of tourists wandering the sidewalks equaled Bourbon Street in New Orleans during Mardi Gras.

"What would you like to drink, sweetheart?"

"Uh, could I see a menu, please?"

"Sure thing."

The server, Betsy, from the name on her denim shirt, didn't move. I squirmed in my chair, a little confused since I'd made it clear I wanted something fast.

"Be happy to bring you one of our specialty drinks while you're deciding on food. We got sweet tea, unsweet tea, sodas, craft beer, daiquiris, and wine by the glass, Cabernet, Moscato, White Zinfandel." She leaned down and whispered, "I'd skip the mixed drinks and wine if I was you."

I took an instant like to her. Betsy wasn't your typical early-twenties employee. Manny's friend must be right. Definitely a former dancer. She wore denim cut-offs and, from the lines on her face and age-spotted hands, she was at least seventy years old. "How about a craft beer," I said. "I'm not fussy. You choose one you'd like. I'm sure I'll like it, too."

"You got it, sweetheart."

She trotted to the bar. Amazing! My legs didn't look that good, and I'm in my thirties. I'll have to ask how she stays so fit. Carefully…didn't want to imply she was old, even though she was no spring chicken.

She brought my beer in a flash. "This is vanilla cream ale. My personal favorite. Take a sip. If you don't like it, I'll bring something else."

I took a sip and fell in love. "Wow! That's really good. Nice choice, Betsy." She nodded and handed me the menu. "Whenever you're ready to order, flag me down. I'll get your food out, ASAP."

"Thanks, I won't take long."

Yikes! I got dizzy looking at the wing choices on the menu. Asian, dry, barbeque, mild, hot, hell, and suicide. I chose to skip those last two categories. Although the blueberry cheesecake fusion wings caught my eye, I settled on medium Jamaican with a honey habanero sauce.

Soon after I ordered, Betsy returned with a small plate of garlic twists while I waited on the wings. The garlic lived up to its reputation. I'd need to avoid close contact with anyone the rest of the day. On the other hand, vampires would not be an issue. I pulled out my tablet. While suspecting nothing short of an exercise in futility, I searched for Carmelita Vasquez, adding showgirl, Las Vegas, Lenny La Mour, and even cruise ship employee. Nothing...zippo.

True to her word, Betsy delivered the wings as promised. "If you need any other sauces, let me know." She smiled and turned to walk away.

Her looks intrigued me. Older, yet in fantastic shape. Her face, while lined with experience, hinted at real beauty in days gone by. "Betsy, do you have a minute?"

She came back to the table and looked around. "Sure, I have a little time. You want to ask me something? Let me guess. Yes, I was a showgirl and proud of it." She kicked her right leg so high it cleared the chair back and landed on the seat. If I tried that, I'd end up dislocating a hip.

"I thought you might be. If you don't mind my saying, you are in spectacular shape. What's your secret?"

She chuckled. "A shot of bourbon and honey every morning, no cigarettes, and an active love life, if you know what I mean."

I probably blushed, surprised by her candor, or maybe I was a little jealous. I steered the conversation back to her professional days. "Did you dance?"

"Oh, yeah, honey, I danced, sang, played the piano, why I performed in bunches of variety shows and musicals. Even did a little burlesque back in the day."

Ah-ha. She was in the right business, I guessed it was around the same time as Carmelita. She may have heard of Lenny, too, if he was as successful as Ruby indicated. "Did you have any long runs with particular shows?"

"I did for a while, but after I reached the ripe old age of thirty, I was demoted to background dancer, even though the young ones couldn't begin to keep up with me."

"That doesn't surprise me." I paused, wondering how to approach my next question. Direct seemed like the best option. "Did you ever work with a performer named Lenny La Mour?"

Her shoulders stiffened. "That scoundrel? He's the one who ruined my career! Said I was too old to be on the front line. He's a cradle robber. Soon as girls turned eighteen, he recruited them for his shows and dumped the rest of us."

Jackpot! What a guy. I wondered why he settled for a sixty-year-old on the cruise. Props to Ruby. "I suppose you won't shed any tears knowing he was murdered a few days ago."

Her shock was expected. But not the tears. "Oh, no!" She covered her face with her hands and shook. "I'd never wished for that. He gave me my start in the business."

I pulled a pack of tissues from my purse and handed her one. "I'm…I'm sorry for your loss." More than a little confused by her second response, I waited until she regained her composure.

She sniffed and shoved the tissue into her shorts' pocket. "Sorry 'bout that. You just took me by surprise.

How was he murdered? Do they have a suspect?"

"Not really, but I would like to ask if you happen to remember another performer named Carmelita Vasquez?"

Her red-rimmed eyes widened. "You mean Debbie Vasquez? Oh, I remember her—very well. She was one of the fresh-faced dancers who replaced me."

Now, we're getting somewhere! "Any idea where she is?"

Betsy hesitated for a moment, like she had more to say. Instead, she shook her head. "Nope. I didn't keep up with Lenny or his girls. I'll ask around, though. You're staying here, right?"

"Yes, for a day or two anyway. Here's my cell number. Please call if you think of anything."

Tears gone, she smiled and patted my shoulder. "Sure will, sweetie. Now, you dig into those wings before they get cold."

I scarfed down the wings and a side of onion rings. *Yes, mother. I promise to eat some veggies tomorrow.* I licked the sauce off my fingers as discreetly as possible before noticing the wet nap package Betsy had placed next to my beer. I wiped my hands, paid the bill—cheap compared to Miami—and left the Spicy Sphinx with renewed energy, optimism, and a possible new lead on Carmelita's stage name.

Just past 6:00 p.m., I wandered through the hotel lobby. Signs advertising various shows lit up the walls. Giant Egyptian statues and palms led to ticket sales and show venues. From magicians to comedians to burlesque you had your choice. On the educational side, a Titanic Museum and Bodies Exhibition drew huge crowds. *Titanic, I can get into. Bodies? Nope.* When it first opened, a few clients had come back with fascinating descriptions of the exhibit, but the thought of mummified bodies and body parts, posed in various positions and states of decay, gave me the creeps.

Tourists swarmed the lobby, waiting for shows to start, checking out restaurants, or wandering into the casino. Never comfortable with crowds, I walked outside for some air. The cabbie had been right. A breathtaking blue light shot from the apex of the pyramid. The Sphinx, taller than the original and in much better condition, lit the sky with a startling orange glow. If your passion was stargazing, however, you'd definitely want to skip Las Vegas.

Contrary to my mid-afternoon arrival, the air cooled rapidly with the setting sun. I wished I had packed a sweater or a light jacket. Close to the equator in Cancun staying warm was never an issue. If I was going to wander around this city after dark, I'd need some kind of wrap. *Great.* My budget was stretched thin enough. I'd rather throw money at the slots for one or two nights than buy a VEGAS "This Is How We Roll" hoodie.

I turned back toward the front entrance. A man leaned against one of the large palm trees. He glanced at me from under the rim of his ball cap. A chill tickled my spine, and the guy sauntered off in the other direction. For a moment, I thought he was stalking me. I chuckled at the notion since dozens of people strolled up and down the strip, enjoying the evening. Still, it unnerved me.

I hurried into the hotel, stepped into the first available elevator, and sped to my floor. Safely in my room, I double-checked the lock and flipped the safety bolt.

Chapter 21

Bzzz. Bzzz. Bzzz. My eyes popped open, expecting to see my South Florida hacienda shutter knockoffs. Instead of the usual latticework light pattern, thick drapes covered the slanted window. Oh, right. I'm not in Miami. Half awake, I located the buzzing sound: my cell phone on the nightstand. Good grief! It was 3:15 a.m. What was it with these middle-of-the-night phone calls? Through bleary eyes, I read, "Private Caller."

Probably Georgia getting payback. "Yeah?" I grumbled.

"Is this Miss Jones?" a female voice whispered.

"That depends. Who wants to know? And can you please speak up?"

She cleared her throat. "You see, I have…I have information for you."

"Information?" I rubbed my eyes, but it didn't dissipate my brain fuzz. "About what?" I waited, but no answer. "I said, about what?"

"You're here to gather information on Carmelita Vasquez, right?"

That cleared the fuzz! I sat up. "Yes, I am. You have something?"

Again, the caller hesitated, and again, she whispered. "Meet me in the Bodies Exhibition in thirty minutes."

"Now? It's the middle of the night! Is the exhibit

even open?"

The woman sighed. "No, the exhibit is not open; however, one of my friends works as a docent, Miss Jones. She sets up private celebrity tours and has access to all rooms. She agreed to help, for a small fee. Now, will you meet me? There's something you need to know."

Sure, I'll jump out of bed and meet some stranger in the middle of the night. "Wait a minute. How'd you get my number?"

"From a mutual friend, and I assure you, I have no interest in doing you harm—only providing information"

"But how will I recognize you?"

Click.

This is nuts! I dangled my feet off the king-size bed and stared at the phone before setting it back on the nightstand. The woman sounded sincere, but didn't all criminals, right before they hacked you into a million pieces and threw you in a dumpster? As if the request wasn't creepy enough, she wanted to meet at the Bodies Exhibition. I pictured the brochure Ellie had shoved in my face. "Good lord," she'd exclaimed. "Imagine seeing all those body parts. Everywhere—body parts!"

She'd freak if she knew I was considering meeting some total stranger there—in the middle of the night, no less. Come to think of it, I was freaked, too. But wasn't that why I flew to Las Vegas? To gather clues? If I controlled my fear, this might be my best opportunity.

I tilted my head from side to side. The cracking and crunching of my neck helped loosen shoulder muscles that held my head in a vice grip. You'd think sleeping on a $3000 pillow-top mattress would make every twinge of back pain disappear. No such luck.

I pulled on the sweats I'd packed for lounging. Catching a glimpse of my reflection in the full-length mirror, I paused. "Andi, you shouldn't be seen in the privacy of your own room dressed like this, let alone in public. Ah, screw it." I squirted a glob of toothpaste on my finger and gave my teeth a quick rub—you never know. Shoving my room card and cell in a lint-filled pocket, I slipped into the hallway. *Here goes nothing.*

To my left, about four doors down, a man and woman were plastered against the wall. Not sure if their awkward movements signified foreplay or an attempt to hold each other up. I turned right toward the elevator, preparing myself for another heart-pounding, claustrophobic adventure. What choice did I have? Stumbling down an empty stairwell in the middle of the night? Not an option.

The use of security cameras, not only in the elevators but throughout the hotel, eased my mind. Not only would an equipment malfunction be detected (God forbid!), but every guest was thoroughly scrutinized. I couldn't help but wonder if some low-paid security officer, feet kicked up, eating a doughnut, was staring into a screen, snickering at the disheveled guest in the baggy sweats.

Never one to pass on an opportunity to act like an eight-year-old, I made faces into the camera until I reached the eighth floor. A distinguished middle-aged man stepped in and glanced my way. I stared at the ceiling, praying he'd ignore my existence.

"Going to the casino?" He flashed a white-strip smile, reminding me I still had leftover toothpaste on my index finger.

"No, I—I just thought I'd get some air. Maybe go jogging." Oh, good, jogging. That would explain the outfit! "Do you happen to know if the fitness room is still open?"

Dressed in sleek navy pants and designer golf shirt, he ran his hand through stunning silver hair. "Sorry. I haven't checked it out yet. Not sure what the hours are, but I suggest you ask at the front desk."

"Great idea," I answered, a little too enthusiastically, and breathed a small sigh when the door opened to the main floor.

"Have a good workout."

"Huh? Oh, yes, and you have a good workout, too. I mean, hope whatever you're doing works out..." *Just shut up.* He smiled and headed toward the lobby's bar.

"That went well." I rubbed the remaining toothpaste across my teeth. Now, to find a bottle of water and make my way to the Bodies Exhibition. Even at 3:45 a.m. the lobby brimmed with guests, some in formal wear, some in cutoff jeans and sweatshirts. And I was worried about being underdressed.

The bar was packed, and the front desk was still busy with check-ins. A tall, striking woman stood on the far side of the lobby, motioning to me. The closer I got, the rougher she looked. Another long-retired Las Vegas performer I guessed.

"This way, Miss Jones." She led me up a set of winding stairs through a double door into semidarkness.

"Thank you for meeting me. I wasn't sure you'd show." She peered back and forth over her shoulder.

I squinted in the semidark room. Not much to see, except shadows of legs and arms in various poses. Despite my brave self-talk, I shivered from head to toe.

I'd guessed the graphic displays were not for the squeamish. With no plans to visit under bright lights, let alone in the middle of the night, I regretted my decision.

"What did you say your name is?"

"I'm Ronni Banks."

She didn't offer her hand, so I kept mine in the pockets of my sweats and waited for some direction.

"I have information that might help your investigation."

"Yes, you said that. Carmelita, or rather, Debbie. If you don't mind, I have a couple of questions. How did you know I was here? And who tipped you off about the reason for my trip?"

"What happens in Vegas…well, you know, Miss Jones. We're a tight community. Your concerns are valid. Wish I could reveal my sources and my motive for helping you, but you'll just have to trust me on this one. Now, do you want the information, or not?"

"I'm here." I shrugged, trying to appear confident. *Maybe she won't notice my knees shaking.*

"Let's go into the office where we can talk privately."

"Oh, so none of the exhibits overhear our conversation?"

She stopped in front of the office door. "I'm getting nothing out of this, Miss Jones. I'm merely trying to help. If you'd rather make sarcastic comments than receive valuable information, then good-bye and good luck."

Guess I'd pushed a little too hard. "Sorry, I'm naturally suspicious, and a bit grumpy when awakened in the middle of the night. Still, you have to admit I have reason to be cautious."

"Maybe it will ease your mind to know Betsy at the Spicy Sphinx is an old friend of mine. She mentioned the conversation you had at dinner last night and your interest in Carmelita Vasquez, and I knew we had to talk. So, if you agree"—she opened a door marked private and flipped on the light— "after you."

"We meet again, Miss Jones."

Under a Miami baseball cap were the haunting eyes of my taxi driver, Diego.

Chapter 22

"Coffee?"

The cabbie, or whatever his true occupation was, handed me a large cup of steaming...something.

"How do I know this isn't spiked, Diego? If that's your real name. Oh, and by the way, I've checked in with the LVPD, a Lieutenant Glass. He's expecting a call from me this morning."

He smiled, flashing a mouthful of white teeth and a brilliant gold crown. Hmmm...cab drivers must make more than travel agents. I could barely afford one cleaning a year.

"I assure you, it's purely coffee. As to your contact with the LVPD, I happen to know Ken Glass. It's my understanding you two haven't communicated since your arrival. Let me calm your fears, Miss Jones. With your permission, I'll be your contact here, and yes, my real name is Diego. Diego Ruiz."

Ruiz? Where had I heard the name before?

He set down his cup and continued. "Please, give me the chance to explain why I asked Ronni to contact you."

Cold fear settled in my stomach. How does this man know my every move? I glanced nervously at my watch: 4:15 a.m.

He must've noticed. "So sorry about the late-night meeting."

"I think you missed *late night* meeting." I gave a harsh laugh. "In my world, it's early morning."

"Yes, well, a matter of semantics and time zones." He sat on the small mahogany desk and gestured toward a chair. "Please sit. By the way, Ronni is my point person and long-time friend. I trust her implicitly, as I hope you will, Miss Jones."

"Rousted from a sound sleep in the middle of the night, or rather, the crack of dawn, you seem to know everything about me, so you might as well call me Andi." I took a swig of coffee and hoped the sarcasm masked my anxiety. *Oh, this is good!* Latte with a double shot of espresso. Diego's value-quotient rose a couple of points.

As if reading my mind, he smiled. "As you like it? Full-fat, of course."

"Yeah, yeah," I responded and slurped a bit too loudly. "It's strong and hot. I'd ask how you knew my coffee choice, but why bother since you know everything else. Before we go any further, however, I do have a question. Were you the man spying on me last night outside the hotel?"

"Yes," he admitted. "If you'll allow me, I'll explain everything."

"Okay, explain away." I sat in a leather armchair while Ronni stood guard by the door.

"One of my oldest childhood friends filled me in on your mission to find Carmelita Vasquez. I understand she may be involved in a murder of which your stepmother is being accused."

"Ruby is not my—" *Why continue to fight such a useless battle?* "Yes, she's my stepmother and, anyway, who asked you to spy on me?"

"Manuel Gonzales and I grew up together in Miami. He didn't ask me to spy, rather assist, and if needed, protect." He paused; I supposed to gauge my reaction. He didn't have to wait long.

My face flushed at the mere mention of the name. "Manny? Uh, Sheriff Gonzales?" My hand trembled slightly when I took another sip of coffee. "You're friends? I thought he was from Cancun?"

"He's worked in Mexico about six years, but we are friends from birth. Were it not for Manny and his family, I probably wouldn't be here today."

Finally, it clicked. "So, you're the private detective friend he mentioned." *Duh.*

"Guilty." He shifted positions, his right leg dangling over the corner of the desk. "We were, and still are, best friends, although our lives took very different paths.

He stood, retrieved a billfold from his back pocket and pulled out a yellowed picture. "We were both thirteen when this was taken. I'm on the left, Manny in the center, and my sister, Gena, on the right. That would be my last happy, carefree day for the next eight years."

I waited for Ronni to chime in, but she stood expressionless, arms folded across her chest, gaze peering down. I didn't know whether to ask about those eight years, or if I even wanted to know. On the other hand, they'd rousted me out of a comfy bed. I deserved a full explanation. "Care to enlighten me?"

"I plan to. That's the only way you'll understand the reason for this meeting." He glanced at the well-worn photo and carefully slid it back in his wallet. "A worthless cousin initiated me into a gang and persuaded me to run drugs. I was too young to know my need to fit in was misplaced with the group of thugs who would rule my very existence from that day on."

"So, how does Manny fit into this?"

"I'm getting to that. Oh, and don't be embarrassed by your attraction to my friend. He's been stealing hearts since I can remember."

With a rush of heat traveling up my neck to my cheeks, along with a sudden ringing in my ears, I struggled to listen as Diego continued the story.

"Manny's father worked as an undercover drug enforcement officer. I was close to eighteen when my cousin and several of his buddies decided to check out a new supplier and invite me along. That supplier was Alberto Gonzales, Manny's father. To his credit, he never batted an eye when he saw me, and I was smart enough to keep my mouth shut."

"But how did you know he was undercover? He could've been a real supplier."

Diego chuckled. "I refused to believe the father figure I'd grown to love and trust would be involved in selling drugs to kids, or anyone. While I'd lost much of my common sense up to that point, somehow I knew to keep quiet and let the transaction play out. Alberto talked to me the next day. I still remember every word. 'Diego, do you want to spend the next twenty years in jail, or do you want to go to college and make something of yourself? Your choice, but you have to let me know right now.' I wasn't sure what he meant until he implied the task force was a few days away from making arrests, but if I swore to stay away from my cousin and his gang, he'd leave me out of it." He sat back down on the corner of the desk. "I suppose you guessed my answer."

"Sounds like you were lucky to be friends with Manny and his father."

"An understatement. Not only did Alberto risk his career and reputation in order to keep me out of jail, but he also helped me get into the University of Miami, with the condition I'd stay straight."

I laughed. "Stay straight? At that party school? Must've been tough for you."

He gave me a wry smile. "Oh, it was hard for both Manny and me, but the consequences of facing the wrath of his father outweighed any momentary pleasure we'd gain from drugs or booze—or women, although Manny struggled more in that area. The girls would not leave him alone."

A flash of jealousy caught me by surprise. "Your story is powerful, but still doesn't explain why you want to talk to me. What does this have to do with Carmelita Vasquez?"

"I'm getting to that, if you will indulge my telling one more family story."

He looked down at his hands for a moment and flexed long, powerful fingers. Fingers I imagined could shatter a windpipe with ease. I mentally calculated how quickly I could make it out the door if necessary.

"My baby sister, Gena, danced from the time she was four-years-old," he continued. "She would put on dance recitals for the whole family, including Manny. If she didn't get at least five encores, we'd hear about it for days. Gena was a pint-size diva. My father thought she'd outgrow the desire to dance, especially after our mother left, but she badgered him until he enrolled her in classes when she was around nine. Because she was so much younger than the rest of us kids, you can understand why she usually got her way. Looking back, it was a mistake, on my part.

"She did surprise us by sticking to the lessons and even getting a grant to study in college. She was well on her way to a successful career until she met a Las Vegas promoter who filled her head full of bright lights and stardom. The worst mistake she ever made led indirectly to her death."

I leaned forward. "What do you mean? Led to her death? How?"

"That's where Ronni comes in," he said. He gestured to the stone-faced woman standing across the room. "Would you mind filling in the rest?"

She moved from her guard position and sat against the wall on a small stool. Twisting the ends of a multicolored scarf draped over her shoulders, she said, "You know I hate talking about this, Diego. I was so fond of your sister."

"Think how hard it is for me to hear, Ronni. But remember, it's for Gena."

She nodded. "I know. I just hate dragging up the painful reminders that led to Gena's death, especially for you."

My neck stiffened. I took a couple of deep breaths to clear my mind and centered my attention on Ronni.

Ronni pulled a small, aluminum-wrapped stick from her pocket and smirked. "Label says this'll control nicotine cravings, but they don't tell you how to control this habit." She popped the gum in her mouth with a harsh laugh that morphed into a coughing fit. "I suppose the gum is better than smoking. Well, anyway, where were we?"

"Gena's death," Diego gently reminded her.

She gave the gum a couple of vicious chomps and continued. "While it was never officially proven, Carmelita Vasquez, aka Debbie Vasquez, aka Little Debbie Dawson, killed Gena." Ronni grabbed a tissue off the desk and dabbed at her eyes.

Little Debbie? My mind shifted to snack cakes.

"Debbie, as she preferred, was a star for years until her age and about seventy-five extra pounds ended her career. Enter Gena. A slender, fresh, mesmerizing dancer. Debbie's husband and manager at the time, Lenny, put her in charge of—"

"Wait! Lenny? As in La Mour?"

"Yeah, they were quite the power couple in Vegas until Debbie's weight ballooned and Lenny lost interest in her, which is when the trouble began. She was insanely jealous when Gena became the headliner of the same show Debbie had produced and starred in for almost a decade."

"Insanely being the operative word," Diego chimed in. "Sorry for the interruption."

"No problem." She spit the gum into a tissue and flipped both in the trash can beside the desk. "Debbie wasn't always crazy. In fact, she and I became friends shortly after she first landed on the strip. I arranged auditions and persuaded Lenny to take a chance on a green, shy country girl straight from a Midwest farm. I owed Debbie everything but watched her become more and more unstable as the years passed. Lenny's infatuation and Gena's newfound fame sent her over the edge."

Ronni opened a little tin and popped a chocolate breath mint in her mouth. "Want one? They help get rid of the nicotine gum taste."

"Sure." I reached into the small metal box and picked out two chocolate-coated mints. "I've never been known to turn down chocolate anything."

Ronni offered one to Diego, but he signaled no thanks. She dropped the metal box back in her bag. "As I was saying, the show, starring Lenny's protégée, Gena, was a hit from the first night, and he was considered a genius for finding her. She was a natural performer, and the better her reviews, the more spiteful Debbie became. Until one night, she snapped. During the final number, Gena was to be lifted swiftly toward the ceiling in an explosion of pyrotechnics. The stagehands pulled her smoothly from the ground. Twenty-five feet in the air, she fell. Police and OSHA investigators found the harness had been tampered with, causing it to break."

Ronni choked up, and Diego finished for her, "Gena died when she hit the floor. Debbie disappeared that night and, apparently, resurfaced five years later on Lenny's ill-fated cruise."

Incredible! "Let me get this straight. You believe your sister and Lenny La Mour were both victims of this Carmelita-Debbie person?" I slumped back in the chair. "And you just happen to be Manuel Gonzales's best friend."

Diego shrugged. "I know it's a wild story, but Manny and I believe there's a strong possibility Carmelita is connected to this latest murder—the one for which your stepmother is being accused."

"For Gena's murder too," Ronni added. "It was never solved. Although everyone in our tight-knit community believed Debbie was guilty." She rooted around in her purse and dumped the entire contents on the floor. "Dammit! Why did I throw out that last pack of cigs?"

I took a couple steps closer to Diego, trusting his neck-crushing ability over the unpredictable rantings of a nicotine-deprived ex-showgirl. I guess, however, I owed both of them a debt of gratitude. Doubtful I would've gotten as much information from the LVPD and Lieutenant Glass. I turned to Diego. Have you done detective work before?"

He nodded. "I've been in the business for years. I'm also a licensed cab driver and make far more at that profession than as a PI. Tips are pretty good as cabby, especially with arriving airport passengers, before they lose everything at the casinos."

"It also provides a pretty decent cover," I added. "You had me fooled in the beginning. I suppose the two murders could be connected, but one thing bothers me. The person listed on the ship, Carmelita Vasquez, wasn't described as being overweight. In fact, Ruby said she was well-built. My stepmother doesn't easily give compliments, especially to other women, so I believe her. Besides, don't members of the ship's crew have to meet certain physical and mental requirements?"

"Well, they have to pass a medical and be physically fit enough to handle emergencies. But as I told Manny, there was no record of her employment. I wouldn't put it past Carmelita's devious nature to purchase fake documents and sneak onto the ship unnoticed."

"There's another possibility," I suggested. "Suppose Carmelita went on a crash diet, or had gastric bypass surgery in order to make Lenny regret tossing her out?" I could see a scorned lover doing anything to get back at the one who'd done her wrong."

Diego nodded. "Possibly. During my investigation, I discovered a probable accomplice."

Now, there's a bit of new information. "An accomplice?"

"Yes, a cabin boy named Hernando Ramirez. According to arrest records, he may be related to her. Perhaps a nephew."

A cabin boy? Could Ethel have passed Ruby's hanky to this Ramirez character? No sense asking if she ever saw him lurking about. Unless a romantic interest came into view, Ruby's powers of observation were nonexistent.

"Miss Jones?" Ronni moved toward the door. "I'm afraid we've spent as much time here as we can without raising suspicion."

"No problem. I need to get some sleep, anyway. I do appreciate all the new information, but is there a way I can get in touch with you?"

Diego spoke up. "It's too dangerous for Ronni, but you may contact me anytime and I'll pass along messages or new tips. You didn't rip my card to shreds, did you?"

"I'm pretty sure I still have it. I do have one more question. Will you be talking to Manny and giving him updates about our conversation?"

He took my hands in his. "He made me swear to call as soon as we spoke. It's almost 7:00 a.m. in Cancun. I'll probably get some coffee in the cafe and call him from there. Would you like to pass along a message?"

I couldn't tell him what I was really thinking. "Just tell him I'm grateful he, and you, have my back."

Chapter 23

Tucked safely back in my room at 5:00 a.m., I collapsed on the bed and fell asleep until 6:15 a.m. when my phone buzzed me awake.

"Andi?"

"Mmmph."

"Are you still in bed? I got tired of waiting to hear what happened with Ruby, so I figured I'd better call you."

"Georgia? Do you have any idea what time it is in Vegas?"

"Vegas? What in the world are you doing in Las Vegas? Oh, Andi, this is no time to take one of your travel agent preview trips."

Eyes clamped tight, I mulled over ways to get Georgia off the phone as quickly as possible so I could sleep for another hour—or four. "Long story short, sis, I got a lead that brought me here. It's just after 6:00 a.m. here, and I've had about an hour's sleep. Can we talk about this later?"

Georgia sighed so heavily into the phone, I braced for wind burn. "Payback's a bitch," she muttered. "No, we can't, Andi. I have appointments today out the yin-yang, and I have to get the kids fed, dressed, and ready to leave in less than two hours. Now, spill it!"

I know when I'm licked. "Can I at least grab something out of the fridge?" A little caffeine was better than none. I stumbled to the minibar, pulled out a cold can, popped it open, and took a long swig. Glancing at the price list, I mumbled, "Hope this is complimentary."

I took another five-dollar gulp and filled my sister in on visiting Ruby in jail, along with Bert, the information I got from Manny, and my early-morning surprise visit with Ronni and Diego. "It was the tip about Carmelita that brought me here to Vegas, and then I find out she was Lenny La Mour's ex-wife and partner. Can you believe it?"

"Barely," Georgia said. "So, do you have any idea where to find her?"

"That's the problem. She seems to have disappeared off the face of the earth."

"And you believe you'll have more luck finding this person than the police?"

I wanted to reach through the phone and flick her on the forehead like when we were kids when she tromped all over my sandcastle the moment I finished building my masterpiece. "I'd hoped you might have a suggestion, or…oh, maybe just an encouraging word. I'm dying here, Georgia!"

"I'm sorry I'm not being helpful. Truth is, I'm full-up with problems and chaos. I'd fill you in, but you wouldn't understand."

"That's uncalled for. Just because I don't have a family and kids, doesn't mean I can't understand how busy you are. You're supermom! I honestly don't know how you do it." And I truly meant that.

Georgia sighed. "I'm sorry, too. Guess I'm just a little jealous of you at the moment. You're building a business, traveling whenever you want, without dragging along strollers, diaper bags, each kid's favorite toy, and four boxes of animal crackers. Yes, they all want their own box. But I shouldn't take it out on you. Tell you what. I'll get Marcus down and try to come up with some ideas. Okay?"

"Uh…sure, sis. Wait a few hours, if you can. I need sleep. Love you."

"Love you, too, Andi."

I hung up, absolutely stunned. Georgia was jealous of me? Go figure. All these years I thought she pitied me because I didn't choose to have a family. "She envies me, and I envy her." I could throw in that tired old phrase, "The grass is always greener," but, I won't.

I fell back on the pillow and slept until 2:00 p.m.

****

Amazing what a hot shower and eight hours of sleep does for a body. I toweled off, slipped into the complimentary bathrobe. *How could I stuff this in my travel bag?* "No time to bring a decent-size suitcase, eh, Andi?" Who was I kidding? Guilt would eat me up.

My first and only experience with "grand larceny" did not end well. I was six. The bounty was a ten-cent pack of my favorite bubblegum. Dad was not amused. "Andi Anna. Please empty your pockets"

Uh-oh.

A five-minute lecture later, Dad and I headed back to the store where I had to confess to the kindly owner I was a common thief. I learned my lesson early. All hotel property will stay with the hotel.

I flipped on the TV and found an old black-and-white detective show, the kind with a good natured, intuitive southern lawyer. It reminded me I needed to call Bert, who was far from good natured and intuitive, and get him started on a lead. "Hey Bert, what's happening?"

"Well, it's about time you answered your phone," he huffed. "I've been calling for the past four hours."

Funny how I just then noticed fifteen missed calls. "Sorry. I had a late-night lead to check out."

"Checking out a late-night lead, eh? Cheating on your sheriff already, Andi?" He let loose with another donkey-bray laugh, making my skin crawl.

"It was a legitimate lead…and he's not my sheriff," I protested a bit too forcefully.

"Okay, okay. Don't get your knickers in a bunch. Say, while I have you on the phone, when are you gonna be back here to babysit—I mean stay—with Ruby? If I'm going to get her cleared of these charges, I have work to do. According to the bail requirements, a responsible person has to be with her at all times."

"A responsible person, Bert? Is someone else there because it can't be you."

Meanwhile, Ruby jabbered in the background, "Oh, Andi, this is just awful. This horrible black thingy is ripping my ankle to shreds!"

I held the phone at arm's length and wondered how to simply disappear into a shadowy Vegas existence. Maybe become one of those faceless showgirls. *Nah. I don't have the stamina.* Spending even one week with Ruby, however, would drive me bonkers, and this trial could go on for months.

Hearing increasing impatience in Bert's voice with his present duties, I hoped putting him in charge of the latest lead would keep him from jumping ship. If he had something useful to do, he'd get off my back. "Bert, I need you to do some research for me."

He sighed. "I suppose that means you're not flying back today."

"No, not today, but I promise, I'll be there as soon as possible. In the meantime, your help will get me back sooner. You may need to sit down for this. And grab a pen and paper while you're at it."

"Just a minute. I think there's some hotel stationery around here somewhere. Okay, done, sitting, spill it."

"You know that lead I came here to check? It concerns one of the ship's personnel, a Carmelita Vasquez." I waited for a response, but Bert was silent, so I continued. "Seems that Carmelita is the ex-wife of Lenny La Mour."

"What?" That got his attention.

"Wait, wait, Bert. Don't say anything that Ruby can hear. She'll freak!"

"No worries here, sugar. I know better."

Finally, we were on the same page when it came to Ruby's hysterics. "I won't go into detail on the phone, but Carmelita, or Little Debbie Dawson, as she was known professionally, had an accomplice named Hernando Ramirez on board the ship. Can you make some calls and look for information online about him? I'd be willing to bet he's no longer onboard, but someone may have knowledge of his present location. Can you do that and still keep Ruby calm and out of the loop?"

"Gotcha. Affirmative to the first part— questionable on the second, but I'll do my best. You have to give me a ballpark as to when you're flying back."

"Soon, Bert. Soon." I hung up before he had a chance to protest.

I considered my options on where to begin investigating Carmelita while checking the rest of my phone messages. Minus the eight from Bert, there were three from Ellie. Darn. Snuggling in to watch an old detective movie would have to wait. I scrolled through the text messages.

—Hey, Jonsey, any idea where you hid those Aruba resort vouchers?—

Delete.

—Hey, Jonsey, I took the liberty to order ten pounds of the chicory-flavored coffee you like. I know what a bear you are before you've had—

Delete.

—Jonsey, how's Vegas treating ya? Anything new to report, hmm?—

Delete.

That left four 888 numbers, obviously telemarketers. I tried to suppress my disappointment that none originated from Cancun. "So, you're too busy to see if I'm alive, huh, Sheriff? Just pass me off to your friend, Diego, huh?"

Diego. A good place to start since he offered to help. Maybe he'd know where Lenny's performances were held. If the club was still standing, which most old theaters weren't, I might find someone who remembered Debbie, Lenny, or even Gena. I pulled out his card and keyed in his phone number.

"Strip Side Taxi."

"Diego?"

"Buenos dias, Andi. How may I help?"

"Do you happen to know if Lenny's last theater survived demolition? I'd like to find someone who knew him or performed in his Vegas act."

"The Lenmour Bar and Casino is long gone, but the structure is still there, and sources say a dance studio just took over. Not sure of the exact address, but it's a few blocks behind your hotel on East Reno. You can walk there but be careful."

I took a deep breath after we hung up, summoning the courage to search Lenny's last haunt. Oh, how I needed a friendly face or voice. I studied the phone for five minutes before hitting speed dial.

"Hola, Andi." The velvet tone at the other end was music to my ears.

"*Buenos dias*, Manny." I wanted to gush into the phone how I missed him and wished I could run straight into his arms. Instead, I said, "Anything new on Ruby's case?"

He hesitated. "Oh, the case. Yes, let me think."

Did I hear a hint of disappointment because the conversation began with a professional question rather than a personal conversation?

He cleared his throat and answered in a business voice. "Señora Jones's attorney called earlier and asked if anyone had interviewed a cabin boy named Hernando Ramirez. To be honest, this is the first I've heard this name mentioned."

I wondered if it was possible Diego had more information about Lenny La Mour's murder than the Cancun police. *Hmmm, that could be a problem.* "I just found out last night, from your detective friend, that Carmelita had an accomplice who might be related. Glad to hear Bert actually followed up on it."

Manny's tone changed. "Ah, so you met Diego, eh? I trust my friend didn't try to sweep you off your feet." He chuckled.

Okay, now I was really confused. Were these two life-long best friends, *muy amigos*, or was I being set up? "Yes and no. We met. He filled me in on a couple of interesting tidbits about Lenny La Mour and his relationship with Carmelita, and that was it. No feet-sweeping."

A hearty laugh came through the phone. "Good. Diego kept his promise."

Diego's promise? What did that mean?

To my disappointment, he quickly moved on. "But back to business. Was your meeting productive?"

"It seemed to go okay, and Diego was definitely helpful, especially in introducing me to an old friend of Carmelita's, Ronni Banks. They told me the awful story about Gena's death."

Manny's voice softened. "Yes, it was tragic. I don't believe Diego's father ever recovered from her death. She was an angel, sent by the grace of God, six years after the birth of the oldest son, Diego. When their mother left, you can imagine how Gena was doted on, or some say, spoiled. I could never figure out why their father blamed Diego for their mother's leaving, but still adored Gena."

"That's terrible. I didn't know…"

He went silent, so I changed the conversation.

"I called Diego this morning to find out about the last known location of Lenny La Mour's nightclub act."

"Did he know?"

"He's pretty sure the building's still there and said I could walk to the location. I thought I'd get some lunch and see if I could spot the place. Diego thinks it was taken over by a dance studio, but he didn't know the name or the owner."

He hesitated. "You are checking it out during the day? Even so, maybe Diego can go with you."

"You're worried about me even in bright sunlight?"

His voice took a somber tone. "Wasn't it daytime when you were last attacked in Cancun?"

Ouch! He had me there. "I don't imagine Diego is worried since he suggested my excursion. So, can I go now? I'm starving."

Manny laughed. "You called me, remember? Please, I would never stand in the way of you and your chicken salad, or turkey burger, or whatever low-calorie indulgences you enjoy."

"Burger, medium-rare with a side of chili fries. Followed by an iced double espresso, just to keep me sharp."

"Please, go eat before you waste away. I'll talk to you this evening, say around nine o'clock?"

"A little presumptuous, don't you think? My evening may just be getting started." Right, like that's going to happen. The only thing I enjoyed more in life than eating was sleeping. "Tell you what, I'll call you one way or the other when, or if, I locate Lenny's former club, or any acquaintances who might remember him. Will that work?"

"Si, call my cell if it's past seven. I'll check out this Ramirez character, just in case he's still on the ship or here in Cancun. Oh, and Andi, be careful. Whoever killed Señor La Mour could be out to stop your investigation—permanently. You've been attacked twice already. Don't make it a third."

I'm glad he couldn't see the smile on my face when he ordered me to be careful. Before the incident at the shop in Old Cancun, I might've brushed off the warning, but I could no longer ignore the threats. "I will, and thanks for…well thanks for caring about my safety."

"Adios, señorita."

I fell back on the bed.

Oh, Manny, why couldn't I snap my fingers and transport you right here, right now?

Chapter 24

Note to self: "Question Diego's 'you can easily walk there' statement."

I walked, and walked, and walked.

I stopped to admire an interesting church and wondered how many hours of the day it was packed with repentant gamblers swearing to never sit at another blackjack table the rest of their lives.

Finally, I came across a three-story concrete building with a faded marquee: DD's Studio of Dance. This must be the place.

It appeared to have been painted turquoise once, although more paint, than not, had eroded from the hot sun and wind. It clearly had seen better days.

"Lenny, if this was your idea of a palatial nightclub, no wonder entertaining on cruise ships was a career advancement."

I walked through remnants of stone pillars leading to a small parking lot and made note of the '80's vintage midnight blue luxury car parked in the driveway. The condition was impeccable, considering its age. I glanced inside at fawn-colored leather seats and spotless interior before moving on. I would have bet fast-food wrappers had never seen the inside of that baby.

I continued up the crumbling walkway toward the ten or so steps leading to the front porch and a new front door out of place on the shabby building. With no doorbell in sight, I took a chance, turned the knob, and walked right in.

An old, but elegant, walnut reception desk dominated the foyer. Definitely a sign of more prosperous Las Vegas days. My impression of Lenny, and his former life, elevated a tad...not much, mind you, but it could only go up.

I studied the intricate wood molding gracing the ceiling and imagined a time filled with brightly costumed showgirls and eager gamblers.

"May I help you?"

My head swiveled toward a petite woman with coal black hair pulled into a tight bun framing large, almond-shaped eyes—eyes ironically the color of almonds. In fact, her whole image appeared strangely beautiful. Although, like Ronni, the closer I got, the older she looked. An aging face, etched with lines, revealed a difficult life. A black leotard and animal-print vest completed the person I assumed was the owner and instructor.

"Sorry for just barging in. I didn't know anyone was here," I said. *That sounded lame.*

"So, I may assume it's your custom to walk in private entrances, unannounced, to steal or vandalize?"

I held up my palms in surrender. "No, no. I'm so sorry I didn't knock, but I just thought this was a business open to the public. Please, may we start over? I'm Andi Jones, and you are?"

"Lillian Ivy." She stood, unmoved, arms crossed. "What do you want, Miss Jones?"

I do believe I've encountered the Ice Queen. "I was told this was once the Lenmour Bar & Casino."

No reaction.

"And that it was owned by a performer named Lenny La Mour. I'm trying to locate someone who knew him or knows how I can get in touch with any of his former employees."

Did her upper lip quiver?

"I don't know anyone by that name. I've only been here for the past two months, and I lease this space from an anonymous international firm, so I'm afraid you're wasting your time."

The increased blink rate of her false eyelashes threatened to lift her off the ground like a drone. I weighed the choice of calling her out on the obvious lie until a sound in the back diverted my attention. "Is someone else here? Did something drop?"

"I'm the only one here. Now, if you don't mind, Miss Jones, I must prepare for my evening class." She ushered me toward the front door in an obvious effort to hasten my departure.

I glanced over my shoulder toward the back room. "But I'm sure I heard a clatter. Are you sure you don't want me to stick around while you check?"

Ms. Ivy opened the front door signaling, in no subtle way, my exit. "Good day, Miss Jones. I wish you success finding the information you seek, elsewhere."

Bam! The door slammed in my face. "Sure you do," I muttered. I debated whether I should look elsewhere or stake out the place. Whoever was hiding in the back room had to leave at some point. Against my better judgment, and Manny's words to "be careful," I had to investigate. Ducking under a window on the left side of the old casino, I made my way to the back of the building. Darn! The only window to the room I needed to check was too high. I did, however, hear voices. Either Ms. Ivy had a habit of talking to herself, or she had company.

Needing just another two feet, I searched the yard for something to stand on. A red plastic crate underneath a small pile of trash caught my eye. I slipped across the yard, grabbed the crate, and set it underneath the window. Climbing on top, I stretched to peek inside. The talking had stopped. No movement in the room. Did they see me?

"Miss Jones?"

Argh! My head spun around, and I lost my balance and fell hard to the ground at the feet of Lillian Ivy.

"May I help you with something, or should I call the police and report a trespasser?"

Between the shock of the fall and being caught in the act, my mind went blank. I scrambled to justify my spying. "I'm so sorry, but I heard voices and thought you might be in trouble…held hostage, or something."

She stared coldly for a few seconds. "As you can see, I'm outside, no one is stalking me, well, other than you, and I'm perfectly safe. Now, please leave, and don't come back."

I took her words to heart and trudged back to the hotel. Maybe Diego could investigate the evasive Ms. Ivy and the dance studio. I didn't dare risk another confrontation.

Chapter 25

I plopped into an empty chaise lounge at the hotel's outdoor pool to gather my thoughts. Guess I should've gone to the room to freshen up, and I wished I had bought that bathing suit in Old Cancun. Wrinkled capris and a nasty mustard stain on my shirt stood out among the sun bathers in stylish pool attire. My backside hadn't touched the seat before a chiseled server stood beside me.

"May I get you a drink, Miss?"

I shielded my eyes from the sun. "I'd like a large, unsweetened iced tea, please, and would you add a couple of lime slices?" Leaning back in the chaise, I pulled out my cell to call Diego. The server hadn't budged.

"I hate to ask, but may I see your room card?"

I placed the phone beside me on the lounge and dug for my card. He swiped it and said, "I do apologize, but we have to be careful. Our guests are—"

"Yeah, yeah, I'm not a trespasser." I hated sounding rude, but I had to get in touch with Diego.

I got voice mail instead. "Can't answer. Leave a message."

Could you sound any colder, Diego? "It's Andi. I really need to talk to you about a woman named Lillian Ivy who has a business in Lenny's former nightclub. You know, The Lenmour Bar and Casino? So, if you

186

can get back to me. I'm on my phone for another hour or so."

I hung up, wondering what to do until I heard back from him. I took a swig of iced tea and looked around. A white-haired man in his mid-sixties, I guessed, leaned on one of the outdoor bars. He was obviously proud of his physique. I, however, couldn't help wishing he'd take himself and his tiny European bathing suit to one of the swim-up bars at either end of the gigantic pool.

I'd finished half my iced tea when a text came in. Good! It was Diego.

—Andi. Meet me @ body exhibit, 1:00 a.m.—

Not again! My worst fear: going back into that creepy museum—in the middle of the night no less. I texted back.

—Can we meet somewhere else, less Edgar Allan Poe-ish—

No response. "Crud."

Gathering my gear, I slugged the rest of the tea and headed back to the room to get a couple hours of sleep before my second late-night meeting. I took a quick shower and dressed in the same warmups I'd worn the previous evening. Throwing the spread back, I plopped on the bed, praying for a couple of hours of shut-eye.

My phone alarm buzzed at 12:30 a.m. Vacationers packed the lobby, same as the night before. Doesn't anyone sleep in this town? I made my way to the exhibit. No sign of Diego. I checked my watch and walked up the stairs in case he was waiting at the top. No sign of him. I fiddled with the door—locked. He still had five minutes to get there.

I walked back down to the main floor and checked out the large posters on the wall advertising the Bodies

Exhibit. A man, arms and legs stretched wide, pink lungs exposed, could've been a singer in a past variety show. Another—all muscle, rib cage, and ligaments—appeared ready to make the winning shot in a basketball game. At least you knew what was inside before you bought a ticket. The visuals reinforced my decision to see as little of the exhibit as possible.

"Where are you, Diego?" He was now five minutes late. I decided to check the lobby, again, when I heard, "Pssst, Andi." A shadowy figure motioned to me from the exhibit landing. I trotted back up the stairs and saw the exhibit door opened, just a crack.

"Come in."

"Diego?" I stepped closer and grasped the right door handle ready to slip inside. Instead, a strong hand grabbed my wrist and pulled me into the dark hall.

Breathe. Breathe. Breathe.

Vertigo hit me—like a thirty-foot wave over a twenty-five-foot cabin cruiser—the moment my eyes peeled open.

An infrared light gave off a glow, dimly revealing a dozen or so shapes within range of my bleary vision. Bracing my elbows on the floor, I tried to sit up, but my arms didn't cooperate. My head slammed painfully to the floor. *Where am I? Think, Andi, think!* Diego left a message to meet at the Bodies Exhibition. I took the elevator downstairs a few minutes before 1:00 a.m. and the rest was blank.

Prickling sensations moved up my legs, and the wooziness subsided. At the very least, some feeling was coming back. I grabbed onto the closest solid object, a wooden stool, and pulled myself to my knees. Minutes passed before I was steady enough to stand and take a couple of steps with support from a nearby metal table. Adjusting to the darkness, I recognized file cabinets, microscopes, and several computers.

I shuffled through a door leading to a smaller room for storage. To the left, a large metal shelf held objects of all shapes and sizes. I took a closer look and gasped. Rejected body parts, or those waiting their turn on the main floor, were stacked in large transparent plastic bins. I staggered back before bumping into a large tub filled with a liquid. From the strong smell, I guessed a type of acid used to prepare skeleton displays.

A large vacuum chamber set next to the tub. I moved closer and read, *Danger Liquid Silicone.* I'd read once in a brochure that human tissue was preserved in a liquid to halt the decaying process— permanently. I wondered if the chamber was occupied. Bile stung the back of my throat. For someone who hates Halloween and suffers from claustrophobia, being trapped in this room of horrors was no holiday.

I stumbled back to the large lab room, grateful I hadn't fallen into the tub. If I could only find a flashlight. *Wait! I have one in my purse. Somewhere.* Crawling on hands and knees, I felt around on the floor for my purse. Nothing. Not only was I drugged and locked in a strange room, my money, credit cards, and phone were all gone.

I wobbled to my feet and felt my way around the perimeter of the room. A faint orange glow to the right revealed a fancy-schmancy keypad. *Ah-ha!* Another door! It was locked—no surprise. That settled it. I was trapped.

Slumping to the floor, my breathing quickened. The walls closed in, threatening a full-blown panic attack.

Outside the door, a female voice sneered, "You're sure she'll be out for a few hours?"

Where had I heard that voice before?

"Trust me. She's out cold," a male voice answered with a Spanish accent.

"I must admit, you handled the guy with precision. He never knew what hit him. Are you up to finishing the job, Hernando?"

"Never doubt me."

Did she say, Hernando? Carmelita's partner? Reality set in. This Hernando guy and his female partner, the elusive Carmelita Vasquez, had come back to finish me. I held my breath, waiting for the click of the lock and bracing for the door to open. But instead, their voices faded.

I exhaled for the first time in, oh, around two minutes. However, my relief was short-lived. First fear, and then rage set in.

Damn you, Ruby! This is your fault! I wouldn't be in this mess if she hadn't become infatuated with a has-been lounge singer. I cursed myself for answering her phone call in the first place. And nearly cursed Dad for marrying her. *Why did you have to die, Mom?*

I'd hit rock bottom blaming my present circumstances on my deceased mother. Enough of the pity party.

I listened at the door for returning voices but heard nothing but dead—pardon the pun—silence. If I screamed my lungs out, what were the odds help would come? The odds were greater I'd alert the two scumbags who locked me in. For now, they thought I was out cold. I'd keep it that way.

I pulled to my feet and tiptoed around the left side of the room, careful to avoid knocking over some valuable piece of equipment. If I could just find a metal tool, maybe I could pry open the main door. A long shot, but I'd run out of options.

My progress stopped when my foot hit a stump—and the stump moved. A corpse-shaped figure was sprawled out on the floor. I threw my hand over my mouth and let out a muffled squeal. I moved tentatively around outstretched legs, praying I wouldn't trip or fall. Just ahead, a large storage cabinet on the far wall looked promising. My spirits raised a notch. Surely in their line of work a crowbar-type object came in handy. After all, human ribs didn't separate themselves.

I took a step forward and froze. A hand gripped my ankle. I cried out and pulled my leg free. I'd heard rigor mortis caused bodies to do strange things, but that grab was straight out of a horror movie. I gasped for breath and slowly backed away.

"H-help."

Nearly passing out, I fell back against the metal cabinet.

"An-di." A pair of familiar hazel eyes stared straight at me.

"Manny!" I dropped to the floor and crawled toward him. "What happened?"

"Don't know," he gasped. "Hit from behind."

My next question should've come first. "What are you doing here?" A few minutes earlier, I would've cheered his presence, but the man sprawled on the floor was in no shape to help. In fact, he was in no shape to move. I took little comfort in no longer being alone.

Dried blood on the floor under his head indicated a

severe wound. "Don't move. I'll try to find a couple of towels."

I stumbled into the small storage room and toward the acid tub to search for anything to stop the bleeding. Snatching several large towels from a nearby metal table, I deliberately blocked images of what might step from the tub needing to dry off. I gently lifted Manny's head and slid two towels underneath for elevation. A quick glance revealed blood matted in his thick hair. "I think the bleeding has stopped," I assured him. "Do you think you can sit up?"

"I'll try."

I placed my arm behind his back and lifted with every spare ounce of energy I could muster. He wobbled but stayed sitting upright.

"I need to lean against something," he murmured. "The room is spinning."

I helped him scoot back against a metal sink and workstation in the center of the room.

"Ah, that's better. My eyes are starting to focus." He reached behind his head and flinched. "Man, that hurts."

I positioned one of the towels behind his neck for support. "Any idea what happened?"

"No. I flew in this evening," he said, his voice raspy. "Diego called the moment he got the text from you. He was working another lead and couldn't meet you. I couldn't stay in Cancun and wonder if you were safe. The last thing I remember is climbing the stairs to the main exhibition hall."

"Wait a minute. What did you say? Diego got a text from me? He's the one who sent the text asking me to meet him. I'd show it to you, but someone stole my phone."

Bleary-eyed, he insisted, "He didn't send it, Andi. Someone must've wanted the two of you here at the same time. They just didn't know I'd be taking his place."

"Considering your injury, they were trying to finish you off. I mean"—my voice dropped to a mumble—"finish Diego off. They almost got their wish."

Manny groaned. "I suppose we're locked in."

"We have to get out of here before they return to finish the job."

He struggled to get to his feet, but his legs crumbled under him.

"What are the chances of figuring out the code?" I asked. "Slim and none, I'd guess."

For the first time, he managed a wry smile. "Guess you're on your own with this one, but I might be able to help figure out the numbers."

I walked to the door, relieved to have more control over my body and mind. Whether newfound strength came from the drugs wearing off or Manny's presence didn't matter. We had to figure out how to crack the code. My first instinct to beat it senseless was my usual way of handling stubborn electronic devices. Shooting it might have worked, but even if I carried a gun, the sound could signal the wrong people.

"How many numbers should I punch?" I asked. "Four, six, more? And what happens if I set off an alarm by pressing the wrong key too many times?"

"Four numbers are normal with keypads that size, and if the alarm goes off, hotel security might be alerted."

I stared at the numbers, zero to nine. What could be

the logical combination? In case those responsible for setting the code weren't too bright, I tried the obvious, one, two, three, four.

"Rats. Guess they're smarter than that."

"Some people use their birth dates," he said. "Obvious and easily remembered, but in this case, we have no idea who put in the code. Do you see any numbers near the box?"

Seconds away from implementing my first idea and smashing it to smithereens, I spotted a note taped on the wall to the right of the keypad: *For assistance type EX 2326.*

"I found a set of numbers next to the door." I pressed the numbers on the keypad and heard a click.

Holding my breath, I waited for the inevitable alarm to blare. Nothing. I whispered for fear of warning our captors. "I think I got it." Cracking open the door, I scanned the hall for movement. Nothing in sight but eerie body displays, and they weren't moving.

I hurried back to Manny. "Can you walk?"

If not, I'd have to leave him there and run for help. Just the thought sickened me but going off on my own might be the only way to save us both.

He staggered to his feet but immediately collapsed. "Go, go. I'll slow you down. Find hotel security." Anticipating my reluctance to leave, he flipped his wrist dismissively. "I'll be fine until you get back."

He had to be. I couldn't possibly drag him around by myself. Racing through the door, I located the glowing EXIT sign at the opposite end of the main room. I sprinted for the main door and threw it open. A menacing woman with a familiar face blocked my escape. *Not again!* Struggling to fight her off, I grabbed her wrist and twisted forcefully, hoping to dislodge the large hypodermic needle in her hand. She screamed in pain. I almost had her when a second person grabbed my arms and pulled me backward across the tiled floor. The needle stopped me in my tracks. The room spun. My eyes opened long enough to see the woman following behind, rubbing her wrist. "Get her back in the room and make sure the other one is dead."

My brain shouted, "Fight back." My body answered, "Not a chance." Despite a second paralyzing drug dose racing through me, I recognized the female in charge. Lillian Ivy. The cold, uncooperative proprietor of the dance studio.

Chapter 26

The partners in crime shoved me through the door of the prep room. I hoped Manny found the strength to hide, or they'd surely finish him off and I'd be next.

Heavy footsteps and a beam of a flashlight moved around the room. "He's not here," Hernando said. "Pooled blood, but no sign of a body."

Lighter footsteps, accompanied by a few choice swear words, moved to the center of the room. "Where is he?" Lillian said. "Why didn't you kill him the first time? You should've thrown him into the vat like I wanted."

"I thought the blow to his head would be enough. He went down like a rock."

She laughed scornfully. "More like a pebble, you idiot! Why I ever partnered with you? You're just like my sister, dull and incompetent."

My breathing sped up. Adrenaline surged through me like water through a fire hose. Either Lillian failed to give me a full dose, or my body developed resistance to her drug of choice. In any case, I had to move before they found Manny. My heart would break if something happened to him. I had to admit an acid bath wasn't on *my* to-do list either.

I crawled on hands and knees, careful to stay out of sight. Lillian and Hernando, seemingly forgetting I was there, continued to argue while they opened every cabinet and searched every nook and cranny.

Hernando snorted. "Maybe he jumped into the tub by himself."

The loud crack of a hand smacking a face was unmistakable. "You idiot! This is no time for your asinine jokes. Keep looking."

I peered over the workstation as Hernando disappeared into the small storage room.

"No one in the tub," he called. "Shelves are loaded with body parts though." He walked back out. "He's not in here. He must have escaped."

Lillian snapped, "Look in the main hall! But first, be sure she's still out cold."

Uh-oh. I crawled back to the door and slumped against the wall. My heart pumped so fast, I couldn't control my breathing. Luckily, they hurried out the door after a cursory check of my state of consciousness. When the coast was clear, I struggled to my feet. The room spun like a merry-go-round. Hanging onto the closest stable objects, I stumbled around the room. "Manny. Manny," I whispered. "Where are you?"

A weak "back here" came from the prep room.

Overjoyed to hear his voice, I wondered how Hernando missed him. I struggled to move; one leg cooperated, but the other dragged uselessly behind. "Where in the world are you hiding?"

As a leg plopped off the storage shelf, I gasped. Next tumbled another leg followed by two arms. Manny slumped to the floor. "Help me to my feet."

"Can you crawl to the tub and pull yourself up? Not sure I'm strong enough. Oh, but don't fall in. It's filled with some kind of acid."

He actually chuckled. "Thanks for the advice."

After a good amount of moaning and groaning, he reached the tub. I helped him stand without either of us falling into the acid bath. "Hang onto my shoulders." I turned toward the door. "We have to get out of here before they come back."

Leading the way, I shuffled toward the entrance to the main hall and cracked open the door to the left. I spotted a light flashing back and forth. "They must be over there in one of the supplemental rooms," I whispered. "We'll have to move to the right."

Depending on me for support, Manny trudged behind as we inched toward the main exit. Keeping an eye on the light movement at the opposite end, we crept behind one body display after another.

I froze halfway to the exit when a beam of light passed over our heads. I squatted down and Manny did the same.

My worst fear was realized when Hernando shouted, "I think something moved over there." The beam searched to the left. We ducked to the right, behind the silicone body of football player being tackled by another.

"Don't move," I whispered. The light wandered above us and then shut off.

"I don't see anyone but the dead," Lillian scoffed. "Your imagination is working overtime. Let's keep looking."

With the coast clear for the moment, I trudged toward the exit. Not an easy task with a two-hundred-pound sheriff hanging on my back. *Just a few more feet.* Focused on the end reward, I failed to hear the footsteps until it was too late.

Lillian waved a small pistol. "Sneaking out on us,

hmm? Take them back to the prep room."

Hernando shoved me on the shoulder, almost knocking me down. "Hey, don't be so rough," I scowled, determined to sound gutsy, even though my insides churned like my grandmother's old washing machine. Hernando grabbed Manny's arm and steered him through the middle of the hall, back to the lab.

A gun shoved against my back, and Lillian's voice came low and sharp. "Keep moving, or you'll end up on one of these pedestals."

I considered making a run for it. Maybe she wasn't that good a shot. Maybe she'd miss me and blow the skull off a skeleton instead. On the other hand, I wasn't ready to lose *my* head. Not yet. Not until I'd exhausted every possibility.

We passed a row of athletes posed to represent each sport. A female volleyball player, a tennis player, a javelin thrower. Without thinking, I snatched the spear and swung at Lillian's arm. Yep, it was real, and thanks to the protective coating, a whole lot heavier than the ones used at track meets or in the Olympics.

She fell to her knees, the gun flying from her hand. Holding her wrist, Lillian writhed in pain. "Hernando, help!"

Before he could react, I snatched the gun off the floor and aimed at his midsection. "Get your hands off him, now! I don't want to use this, but I will."

My hand shook. The last time I remembered holding a gun, I was eight years old and playing cops and robbers with Billy Hodges's cap pistol. I willed my hands to hold the gun steady.

"Hey, don't shoot, lady," Hernando said.

My shoulders slumped the instant Hernando raised

his hands and released Manny. I'd never had to shoot anyone or anything and prayed I never would.

"I don't want trouble. This was all her idea." He pointed to his partner, who was still moaning in pain.

"You already found trouble, buddy." Recovering some strength, Manny shoved the cowardly turncoat toward Lillian. He eased the gun from my hand and held it on the pair of would-be assassins. "Run into the main concourse and yell for security. Yell at the top of your lungs if you have to."

"Are you sure you want me to leave you?" I whispered. "Are you strong enough to handle both of them?"

He nodded. "I'm good, but don't take too long."

I sprinted to the double-door exit. I pushed on the right side. It didn't budge. Fearing the worst, I moved to the left door and pushed with all my might. Hallelujah! I was free!

I ran down the stairs, screaming. My voice must've carried through the lobby, the casino, and every restaurant in the pyramid hotel. Four security guards came running from different directions.

"In the Bodies Exhibit," I gasped. "A man and woman tried to kill me and my companion." I ran back up the stairs, huffing and puffing, with the four officers close behind. Bursting through the door I turned around and yelled, "Don't shoot the tall man with the gun. He's with me!"

In addition to my warning, Manny took no chances. He slowly lowered the gun to the floor and raised his hands. One of the security guards called out, "Keep your hands where I can see them."

"I'm not moving," he assured them.

"Don't shoot." Diego eased through the door, hands up.

"Hey buddy," one of the guards shouted. "You on a case?"

"Hi, Donnie," Diego said. "Yep, this one. I believe you'll find these two are wanted for several crimes, including murder in Cancun."

The guards stayed until the Las Vegas police arrived within minutes. They cuffed Lillian and Hernando, read them their rights, and led them from the room. Manny stared at me with a puzzled look on his face. His mouth moved in slow motion. A far-off voice pulsed through my head. "Andi, are you okay?" I tried to answer, but every speck of adrenaline had drained from my body. My knees buckled. This time, Manny held me.

"Can you make it to the lobby, Andi?"

I nodded moments before I slumped to the floor.

Chapter 27

Mmm...yes, yes. Don't stop. Loving hands caressed my shoulders, and lips gently kissed my throat, moving downward. *Oh, yes!* Hands grasped my wrist and...took my pulse?

"Where am I?"

"You're in the hospital. Sunrise Medical. You've been out for almost twenty-four hours. You were quite dehydrated when the EMT's brought you in, but fluids are doing the job." The nurse let go of my wrist and typed information into a tablet.

I focused on her name badge. "Nurse...Wiley?"

"Yes, you gave us quite a scare. I'll let your visitors know you're awake."

Hospital, fluids, rest, visitors? What had happened? Let's see. Manny and I were in the Bodies Exhibit. The police came. I vaguely remembered being put on a gurney.

"She lives!" Speak of the devil, Manny rolled into the room in a wheelchair. "Nice to see you're awake."

"It's nice to be awake, but how are you? Last thing I remember is being in the hotel lobby surrounded by police. What happened after that?"

"Maybe we can both fill you in." Diego walked in with my purse tucked under his arm. "I thought you might need this."

"Was I dreaming, or were you there when Lillian

and Hernando were arrested?"

He walked to my bedside. "I was there. Just sorry I didn't show up earlier."

"Me, too. You owe me, big time, pal."

Diego laughed. "He'll hold it over me the rest of our lives, Andi. Good news is the doctors say you're both going to be fine and should be released later this afternoon."

What a relief. "Great, but will someone please tell me how I got here?" The overwhelming desire to jump out of bed into Manny's arms would have to wait.

As if reading my mind, Manny moved from the wheelchair to my side. Brushing the hair from my forehead he whispered, "Through no small effort on your part, Señor La Mour's true murderer was arrested. Not your former stepmother, much to the disappointment of the guards at the Cancun police station."

He winced, and we both chuckled.

"Now, if I could get rid of this damned headache." He filled in his side of the story, how Hernando knocked him out at the main entrance.

"All I remember is waking up with a serious case of vertigo," I said.

"Yeah, tell me about it," Manny said and touched the bandage on the back of his head. "The pair left shortly afterward. I suppose to cover their tracks. Guess I drifted in and out until you kicked my leg."

"And you grabbed my ankle. I was convinced I'd stumbled into the *Walking Dead*." Give me a good old-fashioned adventure flick any day. "I'm just happy I didn't have to fire that gun! I was so afraid I'd miss Hernando and hit you."

"You were afraid?" Manny laughed. "I was terrified!"

Diego shook his head, a pained look on his face. "I can't think about either one of you being in such danger. Andi, if you'd rather talk later—"

Manny's smile disappeared. "He's right. You need to get your strength back. We can talk later."

"Good grief, you two are treating me like some delicate flower. I'm fine!" I hollered with enough volume to bring three nurses and two orderlies running.

Nurse Wiley, leading the pack, was livid. "Miss Jones, are you all right or should I ask these gentlemen to leave?"

Shame-faced at my outburst, I answered, a few decibels lower. "No, I'm fine."

She turned to leave, but not before giving Diego and Manny the evil eye. "See that she's not upset again, or I'll kick you two out and insist she stay another night."

"Yes ma'am," Manny and Diego said in unison.

That broke the tension. "Whew! You don't want to be on the wrong side of a needle with her." I said, chuckling. "Okay, I feel better, but please don't stop. I need to know why Lillian Ivy wanted me dead."

"Manny sat on the bed and took my hand. "Because you were getting too close to the truth."

"Truth about what?"

"The killer of Señor La Mour. Carmelita Vasquez," Diego answered.

I threw aside the hospital sheet in frustration before realizing my lovely hospital-blue gown had ridden up a bit too high. Diego and Manny turned politely away, and I pulled the sheet back across my body as subtly as possible to focus back on Diego's tale. "I've never met the woman. How could she know I was investigating the murder?"

"Oh, but that's where you're wrong," Manny said. "After she was taken into custody, Diego determined Carmelita Vasquez had taken the name Lillian Ivy."

"That's what I was doing when your text came in and why Manny showed up at the exhibit instead of me."

"But Lillian looked nothing like the description of Carmelita. She was so tiny."

"In the years after Lenny dumped her," Manny said, "Carmelita found a private clinic that performed surgeries without filing the usual medical reports as long as the patient paid in cash. Within months, she'd transformed into a much different woman, and planned her revenge on Lenny."

Diego chimed in. "Carmelita received a small inheritance from an aunt, which is why she had access to shady doctors."

I tried to keep up, but the information came fast and furious. "I still don't understand. How could she kill Lenny on a cruise ship in Cancun, and then wind up a couple days later in Las Vegas attempting to kill me? I know I'm still woozy. Even so, nothing adds up."

"According to airport records," Manny said, "after Lenny's murder, Carmelita escaped the ship and went straight to the airport. Hernando stayed behind to take care of Ethel and booked a later flight."

"They were both scheduled to fly out together," Diego said, "but unfortunately for Ms. Lipton, they decided the threat of her talking was too great. In a way, Ms. Lipton was a victim of her own jealousy.

According to Hernando, after Ruby was identified to take the fall for Lenny's death, his aunt detected animosity between the two friends and enlisted Ethel to play a practical joke on Ruby. She convinced Ethel the plan was to put Ruby in a compromising position that would make her a laughingstock during the cruise. Ethel thought the handkerchief she swiped from Ruby was only supposed to tie her to a prank. When she found out about Lenny's death, she confronted Carmelita and threatened to tell the authorities. That's when Carmelita cooked up the scheme for Hernando to follow Ethel to the spa, disguised as an employee of the cleaning service. A deadly mixture of chlorine and ammonia led to suffocation."

My stomach churned at the thought of a woman, whose only fault was playing a prank, got caught up in the horrifying scheme. "When I saw Lillian in Vegas, she gave no indication she'd just returned from a whirlwind crime spree. To think, I was alone with her in the dance studio. Wonder why she didn't kill me right there? Especially since Hernando must've been there at the same time, although she swore she was alone."

"Not only was Hernando her partner, but she was also his aunt," Mandy said. "Through complicated family dynamics, she was able to pull him into her elaborate scheme to kill Lenny and frame it on Ruby. As soon as Carmelita discovered Lenny was entertaining on cruise lines, they hatched their plan. That plan meant gaining employment on the same ship."

"Was he the one who attacked me in Bren's Boutique?"

"Yes, he confessed to that, too. He also was the person that shoved you into the bathroom on the ferry. Apparently, Carmelita's sister, Maria, who was Hernando's mother, ran up huge gambling debts," Diego added. Carmelita talked her nephew into helping kill Lenny by promising a huge life insurance payout from a policy she took out years ago on the victim."

I sat up, my head ready to explode. It would take weeks to process the details, but one question remained. "So, how does Ruby fit into this?"

Diego shook his head. "She was in the wrong place at the wrong time. Only by chance did her birthday cruise coincide with Carmelita's scheme to get rid of Lenny. When Ramirez reported Ruby's flirtation with Lenny, they set out to frame your stepmother for the crime."

"My ex-stepmother."

Manny chuckled. "You're going to have to cut her some slack, Andi. She was the victim here, even though her antics and her need to be the center of attention made her appear otherwise."

I had to admit that this time Ruby wasn't to blame. Well, other than for her overactive libido. "I guess you're right, especially since I set all this in motion by booking her cruise in the first place."

I fell back on the pillow, feeling guilty.

"How did Lillian have such easy access to the Bodies Exhibition?" I asked. "Surely they have top notch security equipment."

Diego sighed. "The same way Ronni Banks arranged our first meeting in the exhibit office. It seems a friend, one of the docents at the museum, makes more money from her side job than her regular salary. She's known to let anyone in after hours if the price was right. Carmelita paid the price."

When I first met Lillian, she'd given off bad vibes, but nothing close to murder. My intuitive radar must need rejuvenating. "Did she confess?"

"No," Manny said, "but Hernando was more than eager to get a reduced sentence for implicating his aunt. I don't believe there was much love lost between those two."

Manny's hands covered mine. "Thanks to your quick thinking, and a pretty mean javelin strike, you not only saved us, but two murders were solved. Gena's, along with Lenny La Mour's."

How could I have forgotten the life of the promising young dancer? "I can't imagine how you feel, Diego. Even though it's been years since her death, she'll never stop being your baby sister."

"I'm okay." Diego smiled sadly and stood beside Manny. "You just worry about getting better."

Manny nodded, and Diego patted him on the back, smirking at the sight of his broad-shouldered friend accepting commands. I understood how their friendship had survived for so long.

"I guess it's over, right?" I asked. "Does Ruby know she's been exonerated?"

"Yes," Diego said, "we contacted the Cancun authorities and her lawyer this morning. Mr. Bagley's only response was to ask when you were going to fly back to Mexico to take Ruby off his hands."

We all chuckled.

"That doesn't surprise me," I said. "I don't suppose he asked about me."

He laughed. "No, other than his insistence you call

him, ASAP."

Nurse Wiley stuck her head in the door. "The doctor will be in shortly to see you and then he'll hopefully sign your release papers. It'll be about an hour. Will one of you gentlemen be taking her home?"

"I'll see that she gets back safely," Manny assured.

"Good." The nurse turned to me. "Do you need help getting dressed?"

I shook my head. "Thanks, I can manage." My gaze met Manny's.

I wondered if he was remembering undressing me after my ill-fated margarita binge. My face heated up and beads of perspiration dotted my upper lip. I cleared my throat. "Will you two vamoose so I can get ready to leave?"

Manny nodded. "We'll wait outside but call if you need me. Or us."

I slipped out of bed, careful to keep my lovely, blue-flowered hospital gown in place, and shooed them toward the door.

Diego took the hint and smacked Manny on the shoulder. "Come, my friend. She'll be fine." He turned around and winked before pushing the wheelchair and his friend out the door.

Considerably weaker than expected, I regretted dismissing the nurse. With effort, I managed to gather my clothes and belongings. Standing in front of the bathroom mirror, I cringed. No doubt about it. Manny had seen me at my worst—serious bedhead, no makeup, breath strong enough to fell a two-ton hippo, yet he'd stuck around.

All I had to do is move to Cancun or convince him to move to Miami. I needed to slow down and take a reality check. One crazy evening with the guy didn't mean I wanted to spend the rest of my life with him. *Or do I?* I shivered, remembering the first time I looked into his deep-set hazel eyes. That smile. Those broad shoulders. The tender way he touched my cheek.

"Stop it!" I had to get dressed. The doctor would be in soon, and Manny and Diego were waiting. Slipping into my capris and pulling a T-Shirt over my head took more effort than I'd expected. My whole body ached. *Guess that's the price you pay for catching a couple of killers, huh?*

Diego drove the three of us back to the hotel in his cab. The two lifelong friends sat in the front seat, discussing the facts of the case and what might be next for Carmelita.

It was a tangled mess. I wasn't surprised Ruby fell so easily into Lenny's arms. To her, he was a celebrity, well worth pursuing. How sad Ethel was involved. I could only hope my stepmother learned a lesson.

Right on cue, my phone rang.

"Oh, Andi, honey, are you all right? Land sakes Bert just told me that evil woman almost killed you, too, along with Lenny. Ooooh, my poor sweet Lenny!" She let out a sob and broke into an off-key chorus of some unidentifiable love song.

"Ruby, for God's sake, you knew the man for one night." *Oh, what's the use?*

"Oh, I know," Ruby sighed. "But he was just so dreamy. Well, *c'est la vie*, as the Frenchies say. But how can I live with losing my best friend? Oh, I know Ethel and I had our differences, and I was sometimes insensitive to her feelings, but she didn't deserve this."

I didn't bring up Ethel's part in stealing the

handkerchief that was planted to implicate Ruby in Lenny's murder. Let Bert tell her.

"Now, honey, Bert and I are on the next flight back to Miami. I've packed up the few things you left here and stuffed them in a plastic bag. Just hope I don't lose it at the airport. But from the looks of the contents, nothing would be greatly missed."

There it was. One more dig.

"Well, anyway, honey, I'm just glad you're okay," she added, "and if I have anything to do with it, you'll stay that way. I'm going to see to it you're never alone another minute."

Oh, I don't like the sound of this.

"And since there are no men in your life and none, that I see, on the horizon, I'm perfectly willing to sacrifice my own social life and move in with you for a while. We'll be best girlfriends. Besties, as the young people say." She squealed. My head exploded.

"Wait! Ruby...no."

She'd hung up.

"Problems?" Knowing Ruby was on the other end, Manny's concern was justified.

Problems? When it came to Ruby, problems were the norm. "None that moving to a remote island in the Pacific won't fix."

My only salvation was familiarity with Ruby's lack of long-term commitments. Even if she did make good on her promise to move in with me, I'd give it about two weeks before she found another "Lenny" and left for parts unknown.

"Nothing to worry about," I assured him.

Manny picked me up at the hotel the next morning, in Diego's cab. Before I could ask he said, "The doctors gave me the okay to resume my normal activities. Oh, and Diego said to say goodbye. He was busy or he would've come, too."

Busy, huh? More likely, he wanted to give us time alone.

The ride to the airport was both sad and awkward. The discussion, mostly small talk, edged with long periods of silence since we'd exhausted discussion about Carmelita and the murders. I sighed when we pulled up to curbside check in. "Guess I need to get to the gate since this is the last flight to Miami today."

He smiled. "Yeah, you sure wouldn't want to miss it and have to stay here another night."

I seriously weighed the options. "No," I said, "As much as I'd like to experience Las Vegas as a tourist instead of a sleuth, I've been gone too long as it is. Ellie must be overwhelmed without my help."

An outright lie, but I was afraid to confess my burning desire to jump into his arms and stay forever. Damned adult obligations.

"I know you need to get back to your agency. I'll be here for a few days to clear up loose ends on the case. Afterward, Carmelita and Hernando are being extradited to Miami. I'll be there at least a week giving depositions and working with the Port Authority and the Miami PD." His disclosure was smooth.

"Miami? Why not Cancun?" My breathing quickened.

"Since both boarded in Miami, they'll be taken there to face trial. Oh, and I'll also have a chance to visit family. Didn't I mention my family lives there?"

I pictured my heart leaping out of my chest and landing at his feet. "No, you didn't mention that little piece of information."

"Flight Eighty to Miami is ready to board." The announcement couldn't have come at a worse time.

"Guess this is it." I kissed him on the cheek and turned to walk toward the gate.

He grabbed my hand, pulled me into his arms, and gave me a soft, lingering kiss on the lips. Pulling back, he suggested, "If you're available, I hope we can get together when I'm in Florida, if for no other reason than to test Miami margaritas against those in Cancun."

You can count on it, my fine federale.

A word about the author…

Author Mary Cunningham grew up on the northern side of the Ohio River in Corydon, Indiana. Her first memories are of her dad's original bedtime stories that no doubt inspired her imagination and love of a well-spun "yarn." Through the author's horrifying stint as a travel agent, Andi Anna Jones sprang to life. The mystery series gives extra meaning to the phrase, "Write what you know." Cunningham has several books published, including Cynthia's Attic series, a five-book middle-grade fantasy. She is a member of the International Thriller Writers, Inc., the Atlanta chapter of Sisters in Crime, and the Carrollton Writers Guild. When she gives her fingers a break from the keyboard, she enjoys golf, swimming, or exploring the mountains of West Georgia, where she makes her home with her husband, Ken, and adopted four-legged furry daughter, Lucy. http://www.marycunninghambooks.com

CPSIA information can be obtained
at www.ICGtesting.com
Printed in the USA
LVHW020221010522
717630LV00014B/811